Kim Anna B
Lena-Christin G

Aufgefrischt & wiederholt-Karten Englisch 7/8

Lernrückstände aufholen und Lücken schließen – einfach und effektiv

Auer

Wir haben uns für die Schreibweise mit dem Sternchen entschieden, damit sich Frauen, Männer und alle Menschen, die sich anders bezeichnen, gleichermaßen angesprochen fühlen. Aus Gründen der besseren Lesbarkeit für die Schüler*innen verwenden wir in den Kopiervorlagen das generische Maskulinum. Bitte beachten Sie jedoch, dass wir in Fremdtexten anderer Rechtegeber*innen die Schreibweise der Originaltexte belassen mussten.
In diesem Werk sind nach dem MarkenG geschützte Marken und sonstige Kennzeichen für eine bessere Lesbarkeit nicht besonders kenntlich gemacht. Es kann also aus dem Fehlen eines entsprechenden Hinweises nicht geschlossen werden, dass es sich um einen freien Warennamen handelt.

In den digitalen Zusatzmaterialien sind PDF-Dateien enthalten. Weitere Informationen entnehmen Sie bitte der beigefügten Liesmich.txt.

1. Auflage 2022

Autor*innen: Kim Anna Bachmann, Lena-Christin Grzelachowski
Coverillustration: Carla Miller
Illustrationen: Corina Beurenmeister, Heike Heimrich, Julia Flasche, Kristina Klotz, Steffen Jähde, Tina Pohl
Satz: fotosatz griesheim GmbH
Druck und Bindung: Joh. Walch GmbH & Co. KG, Augsburg
ISBN 978-3-403-**08729**-8
www.auer-verlag.de

Inhaltsverzeichnis

Tenses

- Simple present 7
- Present progressive 9
- Simple past 11
- Present perfect 13
- Past perfect 15
- Present perfect progressive 17
- Will-future 19
- Going to-future 21
- "To be" in the simple present and in the simple past 23
- Simple present or present progressive 25
- Simple past or present perfect 27
- Simple past or past perfect 29
- Present perfect or present perfect progressive 31
- Will-future or going to-future 33

Parts of Speech

- Adjectives and adverbs 35
- Comparison of adjectives and adverbs 37
- Possessive pronouns 39
- Reflexive pronouns 41
- Reciprocal pronouns 43
- Relative clauses – who, which, that 45
- Relative clauses – whose, whom 47
- If-clauses – type I 49
- If-clauses – type II 51
- If-clauses – type III 53
- Active and passive voice 55
- Active and passive in the simple present 57
- Active and passive in the simple past 59
- Active and passive in the present perfect 61
- Active and passive in the past perfect 63
- Gerund as a subject 65
- Gerund as an object 67
- Gerund after a preposition 69
- Modal auxiliaries 71

Inhaltsverzeichnis

Reading

- Pre-reading activity – the heading and the picture 73
- Skimming 75
- Scanning 77
- Detailed reading 79

Writing

- Writing about your holiday destination 81
- Writing an e-mail 83
- Writing a formal and an informal letter 85
- Writing a report 87
- Writing a blog entry 89
- Giving advice 91
- Structuring your opinion 93
- Supporting your argument 95
- Disagreeing with an argument 97

Vocabulary

- Study tips 99
- Useful phrases for the classroom 101
- Differences between British and American English 103
- Common vocabulary in British and American English 105
- 25/5 method 107
- Word map 109
- Record – play – repeat 111

Die Benutzerhinweise zum Download des Zusatzmaterials und den entsprechenden Zusatzcode finden Sie auf der letzten Karte.

Vorwort

Liebe Kolleg*innen,
wer kennt es nicht? Bedingt durch Krankheiten, Unterrichtsausfall, Ferien, Ausflüge oder Klassenfahrten ist die Lernzeit oft sehr kurz und man wünscht sich, mehr Zeit zur Verfügung zu haben, um wichtige Themen noch einmal aufzufrischen und mit der Klasse wiederholen zu können. Man sucht in verschiedenen Büchern und Heften Arbeitsblätter zusammen, kopiert sie für jeden und merkt dann, dass es Lernende gibt, die lieber andere Themengebiete wiederholen sollten und diese Aufgaben teils überflüssig für sie waren.
An diesen Leitgedanken knüpft dieses Werk an, daher auch der Titel „Aufgefrischt & wiederholt". Mit diesen Karten werden die wichtigsten Themen, die Ihre Klasse auch als Grundlage für die höheren Jahrgangsstufen benötigt, aufgefrischt und wiederholt. Die Schüler*innen können dabei ganz individuell an ihren Defiziten arbeiten. Es gibt zwei verschiedene Möglichkeiten:

1. Sie als Lehrkraft legen fest, welche Themen die einzelnen Schüler*innen bearbeiten sollen.
2. Der*die Schüler*in legt selbst fest, in welchen Bereichen er*sie eine Auffrischung benötigt. Diese Variante bietet sich natürlich erst dann an, wenn die Schüler*innen gut selbstreflektieren können.

Die Karten sind immer gleich aufgebaut: Auf der Vorderseite steht die Erklärung, auf der Rückseite sind passende Aufgaben vorhanden. Mithilfe der Lösungskarten im digitalen Zusatzmaterial, das Sie über den Code auf der letzten Karte herunterladen können, kontrollieren die Schüler*innen ihre Lösungen. Dieses selbstständige Arbeiten sowie das Format wirken zudem motivierend auf die Schüler*innen.
Für den Gebrauch im Unterricht bietet es sich an, dass jede*r Lernende ein eigenes Heft für diese Karten zur Verfügung hat. Dieses bleibt in der Schule. Um eine gute Übersicht zu bekommen, was die Schüler*innen bearbeiten, können Sie im Vorfeld eine Tabelle mit den Überschriften der Karten erstellen und die Namen Ihrer Schüler*innen eintragen. Diese können dann nach der Bearbeitung und Korrektur passend einen Haken setzen.
Die Karten sind frei im Unterricht einsetzbar. Möglich ist beispielsweise jeden Tag der Einsatz für 10 bis 15 Minuten oder in einer bestimmten vorgegebenen Lernzeit. Auch in Vertretungsstunden kann natürlich daran gearbeitet werden.
Wir wünschen Ihnen und Ihren Lernenden viel Freude mit diesen Karten!

Ihre Kim Anna Bachmann und Lena-Christin Grzelachowski

EXPLANATION: SIMPLE PRESENT

Wann wird das ***simple present*** verwendet?

➜ Wenn man von Ereignissen spricht, die **regelmäßig oder nie** stattfinden.
We never eat pancakes.

➜ Wenn man von **Tatsachen** spricht.
My family lives in Germany.

Beachte im *simple present* immer die Regel:

Beachte: *I do, you do, he/she/it does, we do, you do, they do*

Verneinungen werden mit ***do/does + not + infinitive*** gebildet.
Fragen werden mit ***do/does + infinitive*** gebildet.

Beispiele: *The kids* ***don't like*** *broccoli. / Marco* ***doesn't like*** *broccoli.*
Do *the kids* ***like*** *broccoli? /* ***Does*** *Marco* ***like*** *broccoli?*

Signalwörter:
always (immer), *sometimes* (manchmal), *often* (oft/häufig), *never* (nie), *usually* (in der Regel), *every day/week/month/year/…* (jede/n/s Tag/Woche/Monat/Jahr/…)

SIMPLE PRESENT

1. Copy the text below into your exercise book.
a) Underline the signal words for the simple present in blue.
b) Put the verbs in the correct form of the simple present!

Marco and John ________________ (go) to school together every morning. They usually ________________ (go) by bus but not on Tuesdays. Every Tuesday John's sister Rebecca ________________ (take) them to school in her new car. On Tuesdays she ________________ (work) in a deli near school. The boys ________________ (enjoy) the ride to school very much. They ________________ (like) to go to school by car, but they ________________ (not like) to go to school by bus. Rebecca ________________ (not enjoy) taking the boys to school. She ________________ (think) that they are annoying.

2. Form three questions based on the text above and answer them. The example helps you!

What do Marco and John enjoy?

They enjoy that Rebecca takes them to school.

EXPLANATION: PRESENT PROGRESSIVE

Wann wird das ***present progressive*** (auch ***present continuous***) verwendet?

➜ Wenn man von einem **Ereignis** berichtet, das **in dieser Sekunde** stattfindet (und gegebenenfalls über einen bestimmten Zeitraum andauert). (Jetzt-Zeit)
The girls are walking on the street.
I am watching a movie now.

➜ Wenn eine **Handlung** nur **vorübergehend** stattfindet.
Rebecca is working in the deli during the holidays.

Das *present progressive* wird wie folgt gebildet: ***am/are/is + ing form***

Beachte: *I am, you are, he/she/it is, we are, you are, they are*

Verneinungen werden mit ***am/are/is + not + ing form*** gebildet.
Fragen werden mit ***am/are/is + ing form*** gebildet.

Beispiele: *The two boys **aren't working**./Marco **isn't working** in the deli.*
***Are** the two boys **working**?/**Is** Marco **working** in the deli?*

Signalwörter:
just (gerade), *still* (immer noch), *now* (jetzt), *at the moment* (in diesem Moment), *Look!* (Schau!), *Listen!* (Hör zu!), *(right) now* (jetzt)

PRESENT PROGRESSIVE

1. Copy the text below into your exercise book.
a) Underline the signal words for the present progressive in blue.
b) Put the verbs in the correct form of the present progressive!

Rebecca ________________ (work) in the deli. She ________________ (make) sandwiches at the moment. Right in this second two young men ________________ (enter) the deli. They ________________ (stand) in front of the bar and ________________ (look) at the menu now. Rebecca ________________ (watch) them. She thinks that the boy who ________________(talk) at this moment is cute. Rebecca ________________ (walk) to the bar to take the order. The two boys ________________ (order), and Rebecca ________________ (think) about asking the boy for his number. While the boys ________________ (eat) she can't stop looking at him. The cute boy gets up and asks, "Why ________________ you ________________ (look) at me? Do you want my phone number?" "Of course!" she says.

2. Form three questions based on the text and answer them. The example helps you!

> Where is Rebecca working?

> She is working in the deli.

EXPLANATION: SIMPLE PAST

Wann wird das ***simple past*** verwendet?

➜ Wenn man von einem **Ereignis** spricht, das in der **Vergangenheit** liegt und **abgeschlossen** ist.
Rebecca worked in the deli yesterday.

➜ Wenn man eine **Geschichte** erzählt oder schreibt.
Once upon a time there was a big castle …

Im ***simple past*** unterscheidet man zwischen **zwei Verbformen**:

Bei **regelmäßigen Verben** lautet die Regel **infinitive + -ed**. Beispiel: *The boys played games.*	**Unregelmäßige Verben** muss man **auswendig lernen**. Beispiel: *John went to school by bus.*

Verneinungen werden mit ***did + not + infinitive*** gebildet.
Fragen werden mit ***did + infinitive*** gebildet.

Beispiele: *The boys **didn't work** in the deli./Rebecca **didn't work** in the deli.*
***Did** the boys **work** yesterday?/**Did** Rebecca **work** yesterday?*

Signalwörter:
yesterday (gestern), *last week/month/year/…* (letzte/n/s Woche/Monat/Jahr/…), … *ago* (vor …), *in 1985* (im Jahr 1985), *the other day* (letztens)

SIMPLE PAST

1. Copy the text below into your exercise book.
a) Underline the signal words for the simple past in blue.
b) Put the verbs in the correct form of the simple past!

Marco and John ________________ (go) to New York during their last summer holidays. They ________________ (have) a great time, and ________________ (enjoy) it a lot. The weather ________________ (be) sunny most of the time, and it only ________________ (rain) once while they ________________ (be) there. Marco ________________ (not like) the big city, but John ________________ (love) it. They ________________ (see) many sights there. They ________________ (visit) the Empire State Building and Ground Zero, but they ________________ (not see) much of Central Park because it is so big. Marco ________________ (like) the New York delis the most. John ________________ (not like) the food in one deli because they ________________ (not have) a vegetarian menu. It ________________ (not be) easy for him to find good food at that place. Therefore, the boys ________________ (decide) not to go there again. All in all, John and Marco ________________ (enjoy) the trip last summer very much.

2. Form three questions based on the text and answer them. The example helps you!

Did John and Marco go to California?

No, they didn't. They went to New York.

EXPLANATION: PRESENT PERFECT

Wann wird das ***present perfect*** verwendet?

➜ Wenn ein **Ereignis** in der **Vergangenheit abgeschlossen** wurde, aber die **Folgen bis in die Gegenwart** reichen.
I have left you the shopping list on the kitchen table.

➜ Wenn ein Ereignis in der **Vergangenheit begann** und **bis jetzt andauert**.
I have lived in Germany for 15 years.

➜ Wenn eine **Handlung gerade** erst **beendet** wurde.
She has just finished her homework.

Das *present perfect* wird wie folgt gebildet: ***have/has + past participle***

Beachte: *I have, you have, he/she/it has, we have, you have, they have*

Verneinungen werden mit ***have/has + not + past participle*** gebildet.
Fragen werden mit ***have/has + past participle*** gebildet.

Beispiele: *I **haven't done** my homework yet./She **hasn't done** her homework yet.*
***Have** you **done** your homework yet?/**Has** she **done** her homework yet?*

Signalwörter:
already (bereits), *recently* (vor Kurzem), *never* (niemals), *up to now* (bis jetzt), *just* (gerade), *ever* (je), *yet* (noch), *not yet* (noch nicht), *for* (für …), *since* (seit …)

PRESENT PERFECT

1. Copy the text below into your exercise book.
a) Underline the signal words for the present perfect in blue.
b) Put the verbs in the correct form of the present perfect!

Rebecca ______________ (have) a stressful day in the deli. It was very busy, and she ______________ just ______________ (get) home from work. Rebecca ______________ (not stop) thinking about the cute boy ever since she met him. John and Marco ______________ (call) Rebecca for four hours now, but Rebecca ______________ just ______________ (see) it. She calls them back, and Marco picks up the phone. He says, "Hi Rebecca, guess who we ______________ (be) with for the last four hours? Yes, we ______________ (be) with the cute guy who you met in the deli this afternoon. He won't stop talking about you. You can come over. We are at the mall." Rebecca says, "I ___________ (hope) for something like this to happen. I will be there in 30 minutes!"

2. Form questions out of the sentences and answer them.
1) Rebecca has had a boring day in the deli.
2) Rebecca has stopped thinking about the boy.
3) John and Marco have called Rebecca for four hours.

EXPLANATION: PAST PERFECT

Wann wird das ***past perfect*** verwendet?

➜ Wenn man ein **Ereignis** beschreibt, das **vor einem abgeschlossenen Ereignis** in der Vergangenheit erfolgt ist.
I did my homework after I had watched TV.

Das *past perfect* wird häufig mit dem ***simple past*** in einem Satz angewandt. Es wird auch als **Vorvergangenheit** bezeichnet.

Das *past perfect* wird wie folgt gebildet: ***had + past participle***

Verneinungen werden mit ***had + not + past participle*** gebildet.
Fragen werden mit ***had + past participle*** gebildet.

Beispiele: *The boys **hadn't been** to Greece until they won the journey. /*
*She **hadn't been** to Greece until she won the journey.*
***Had** they **been** to Greece before?/**Had** she **been** to Greece before?*

Signalwörter:
when (als), *before* (bevor), *after* (nachdem), *never* (niemals), *once* (einmal), *as soon as* (sobald)

PAST PERFECT

1. Copy the text below into your exercise book.
a) Underline the signal words for the past perfect in blue.
b) Put the verbs in the correct form of the past perfect!

John had some crazy days. It all started on Monday when he ________________ (miss) the bus. After his mum ________________ (take) him to school, he realized that he ________________ (forget) his homework on his desk. What a day! Tuesday was rather relaxing. After Rebecca ________________ (take) him and Marco to school, they enjoyed a regular school day. But after school things went crazy! As soon as John's friends Benny and Steven ________________ (arrive) at his house, they had a great time at the pool. They ________________ never ________________ (stay) at his house before, but on that day they all had a sleep over. After they ________________ (decide) what movie to watch, they had a great argument about what to eat for dinner. They had a great time and they enjoyed it a lot!

2. Form three questions based on the text and answer them. The example helps you!

Had John missed the bus on Monday morning?

Yes, he had.

EXPLANATION: PRESENT PERFECT PROGRESSIVE

Wann wird das ***present perfect progressive*** verwendet?

➜ Wenn man ein **Ereignis** oder eine **Handlung** beschreibt, welches/welche in der **Vergangenheit begann** und bis in die **Gegenwart andauert** oder **kurz vorher endete**.
My family has been living in Munich since 2019.

Das *present perfect progressive* verdeutlicht, dass das Ereignis über einen **bestimmten Zeitraum** hinweg stattfindet oder stattgefunden hat. Die **Dauer** des Ereignisses steht somit im Vordergrund.

Das *present perfect progressive* wird wie folgt gebildet: ***have/has + been + ing form***

Beachte: *I have, you have, he/she/it has, we have, you have, they have*

Verneinungen werden mit ***have/has + not + been + ing form*** gebildet.
Fragen werden mit ***have/has + been + ing form*** gebildet.

Beispiele: *I **haven't been feeling** well since I came here./He **hasn't been feeling** well since he came here.*
***Has** she **been doing** her homework for three hours now?/**Have** you **been doing** your homework for three hours now?*

Signalwörter:
since (seit), *for* (für), *all day/week/month (den ganzen Tag/die ganze Woche/den ganzen Monat)*

PRESENT PERFECT PROGRESSIVE

1. Copy the text below into your exercise book.
a) Underline the signal words for the present perfect progressive in blue.
b) Put the verbs in the correct form of the present perfect progressive!

John, Marco, Rebecca, Ben and Steven ________________ (have) a busy day.

Here is what they ________________ (do) all day:

John ________________ (work) on his science project for school since the evening.

Marco ________________ (help) John for about three hours.

John and Marco ________________ (study) the whole afternoon.

Rebecca ________________ (talk) on the phone to her best friend Amy all day.

Ben and his mom ________________ (do) a lot of work in the garden the whole day.

Steven ________________ (watch) his favourite series all Saturday. He loves it!

2. Form three questions based on the text and answer them. The example helps you!

Has John been working in the garden with his mom?

No, he hasn't.

EXPLANATION: WILL-FUTURE

Wann wird das ***will-future*** verwendet?

➜ Wenn man eine **spontane Entscheidung** trifft.
This shirt looks really nice. I will buy it.

➜ Wenn man **Versprechen, allgemeine Vorhersagen, Vermutungen** und **Hoffnungen** formuliert.
I promise I will help you next week.
I will be 30 in March.
I think we will have a great time and much fun.
I hope Jake will be there, too.

Das *will-future* wird wie folgt gebildet: ***will + infinitive***

Verneinungen werden mit ***will + not + infinitive*** gebildet.
Fragen werden mit ***will + infinitive*** gebildet.

Beispiele: *I hope that my family and I* ***won't forget*** *the sandwiches at home.*
Will *the weather* ***be*** *good?*

Signalwörter:
tomorrow (morgen), *soon* (bald), *in the future* (in der Zukunft), *next week/month/year/Saturday/…* (nächste/n/s Woche/Monat/Jahr/Samstag/…)

Die Signalwörter im will-future und im going to-future sind gleich. Aus diesem Grund entscheidet der Inhalt des Satzes darüber, welche Zeitform verwendet wird.

WILL-FUTURE

1. Copy the text below into your exercise book.
Put the verbs in the correct form of the will-future!

Rebecca and Amy have just decided that they ________________ (go) to the park later. They hope the sun ________________ (shine), and that it ________________ (not rain) today. Rebecca has promised Amy that she ________________ (bring) her skates, so that they can skate in the park. There hopefully ________________ (not be) too many people later, so that they have more space to skate. Amy thinks that they ________________ (have) a great time together. They probably ________________ (talk) a lot and ________________ (have) a lot of fun. Amy promised that she ________________ (not be) late today, and Rebecca really hopes that she ________________ (be) on time because Amy is usually late. The two girls are sure that they ________________ (make) great memories together.

2. Form three questions based on the text and answer them. The example helps you!

Where will Rebecca and Amy go today?

They will go to the park.

EXPLANATION: GOING TO-FUTURE

Wann wird das ***going to-future*** verwendet?

➜ Wenn man von **festen Plänen** spricht, die man für die **Zukunft** hat.
I am going to visit my grandparents next summer.

➜ Wenn **absehbar** ist, was passieren wird (**logische Schlussfolgerung**).
I am going to get a good report card because I studied a lot.

Das *going to-future* wird wie folgt gebildet: ***am/are/is + going to + infinitive***

Beachte: *I am, you are, he/she/it is, we are, you are, they are*

Verneinungen werden mit ***am/are/is + not + going to + infinitive*** gebildet.
Fragen werden mit ***am/are/is + going to + infinitive*** gebildet.

Beispiele: *He **isn't going to come** to the party next week.*
***Are** we **going to go** to the adventure park next weekend?*

Signalwörter:
tomorrow (morgen), *soon* (bald), *in the future* (in der Zukunft), *next week/month/year/Saturday/…*
(nächste/n/s Woche/Monat/Jahr/Samstag/…)

Die Signalwörter im will-future und im going to-future sind gleich. Aus diesem Grund entscheidet der Inhalt des Satzes darüber, welche Zeitform verwendet wird.

GOING TO-FUTURE

1. Copy the text below into your exercise book.
Put the verbs in the correct form of the going to-future!

Ben and Steven ________________ (meet) next weekend because they ________________ (plan) the next summer holidays together. Before that Ben and Steven create a list of holiday plans.

Ben ________________ (visit) his grandparents in Wales. He thinks that Steven ________________ (come) with him in the first week of the summer holidays. But Steven ________________ (not join) Ben because he ________________ (go) to the adventure park with John.

In the second week Steven and Ben ________________ (be) in a football camp.

In the third week of the upcoming holidays the boys ________________ (not see) their families because they ________________ (travel) to Dublin.

2. Form three questions based on the text and answer them. The example helps you!

Who is Ben going to visit?

He is going to visit his grandparents.

EXPLANATION: "TO BE" IN THE SIMPLE PRESENT AND IN THE SIMPLE PAST

Das **Verb (*to*) *be* verändert sich** je nachdem, um welche Person/Personen oder Sache/Sachen es geht.

simple present		***simple past***	
positive	***negative***	***positive***	***negative***
I am/I'm	*I am not/I'm not*	*I was*	*I was not/wasn't*
you are/you're	*you are not/you aren't*	*you were*	*you were not/you weren't*
he is/he's	*he is not/he isn't*	*he was*	*he was not/he wasn't*
she is/she's	*she is not/she isn't*	*she was*	*she was not/she wasn't*
it is/it's	*it is not/it isn't*	*it was*	*it was not/it wasn't*
we are/we're	*we are not/we aren't*	*we were*	*we were not/we weren't*
you are/you're	*you are not/you aren't*	*you were*	*you were not/you weren't*
they are/they're	*they are not/they aren't*	*they were*	*they were not/they weren't*

"TO BE" IN THE SIMPLE PRESENT AND IN THE SIMPLE PAST

1. Copy the text below into your exercise book.
a) Underline the signal words for the simple present in blue.
b) Underline the signal words for the simple past in green.
c) Fill in the correct form of the verb "to be" in the simple present or the simple past!

Rebecca and Amy ________________ at the mall yesterday. They ________________ usually together every Monday to do something cool. Amy ________________ (not) happy yesterday because she has had such a bad day. She ________________ at the university in the morning, and she forgot all her papers. Later she ________________ in the city centre for a job interview, but it didn't go well. Rebecca ________________ happy because she has had a great day, so she decided to cheer Amy up. Rebecca ________________ happy almost every day. Yesterday she has had a good day because she ________________ in the deli, and everything went well. Rebecca and Amy ________________ best friends, so they enjoy their time together very much. Rebecca ________________ very good at cheering Amy up, so at the end of the day the girls had a lot of fun. At first Amy ________________ unhappy, but in the end she felt fine.

EXPLANATION: SIMPLE PRESENT OR PRESENT PROGRESSIVE

Wenn **mehr als eine Zeitform** Anwendung findet, sollte man den **Inhalt** des Textes genau verstehen und mithilfe von **Signalwörtern** entscheiden, welche Zeitform angewandt werden soll.

	simple present	***present progressive***
Wann?	➜ Ereignisse, die **regelmäßig** stattfinden ➜ Ereignisse, die **nie** stattfinden ➜ **Tatsachen**	➜ Ereignisse, die jetzt **in diesem Moment** stattfinden (und ggf. über einen bestimmten Zeitraum andauern) ➜ Handlungen, die nur **vorübergehend** stattfinden
Wie?	➜ ***he, she, it* – das -s muss mit!** ➜ ansonsten Verb im Infinitiv ➜ **Verneinungen** mit dem Hilfsverb ***don't/doesn't*** ➜ **Fragen** mit dem Hilfsverb ***do/does***	➜ ***have/has + past participle*** ➜ **Verneinungen** mit ***haven't/hasn't + past participle*** ➜ **Fragen** mit ***have/has + past participle***
Signal-wörter	➜ *always, sometimes, often, never, usually, every day/week/month/year/…*	➜ *(right) now, just, at the moment, Look!, Listen!, still, this week*

SIMPLE PRESENT OR PRESENT PROGRESSIVE

1. Copy the text below into your exercise book.

a) Underline the signal words for the simple present in blue.
b) Underline the signal words for the present progressive in green.
c) Fill in the correct form of the simple present or the present progressive!

Rebecca ________________ (meet) her friend Jennifer every Friday. They usually ________________ (go) to the cinema together but not today. The two girls ________________ (stand) in front of the cinema now, but it ________________ (be) closed. At the moment they ________________ (wonder) why they can't watch a movie like they usually ______________ (do). Rebecca ________________ (say), "Listen! I ________________ (get) an idea! We could go to the diner and meet Jeff and Luke." Jennifer ________________ (not want) to go to the diner because she ________________ (not like) Jeff very much. Jennifer ________________ (suggest), "Let's ________________ (go) to the park like we often________________ (do)." Rebecca ________________ (agree). The sun ________________ (shine) now. Right now the girls ________________ (eat) ice cream and ________________ (look) at some old pictures on their cell phones. "Look! We ________________ (have) so much fun in this picture!" "We never ________________ (go) to the park on Fridays," says Rebecca. The girls ________________ (decide) to go to the park more often from now on.

EXPLANATION: SIMPLE PAST OR PRESENT PERFECT

Wenn **mehr als eine Zeitform** Anwendung findet, sollte man den **Inhalt** des Textes genau verstehen und mithilfe von **Signalwörtern** entscheiden, welche Zeitform angewandt werden soll.

	simple past	***present perfect***
Wann?	➜ **abgeschlossene Ereignisse** aus der Vergangenheit (Geschichten / Informationen)	➜ Ereignisse, die in der **Vergangenheit** liegen und bis in die **Gegenwart andauern** oder **Auswirkungen** auf die Gegenwart haben ➜ Handlungen, die **gerade** erst **beendet** wurden
Wie?	➜ regelmäßige Verben: ***infinitive + ed*** ➜ unregelmäßige Verben: **müssen auswendig gelernt werden** ➜ **Verneinungen** mit dem Hilfsverb ***didn't*** ➜ **Fragen** mit dem Hilfsverb ***did***	➜ ***have/has + past participle*** ➜ **Verneinungen** mit ***haven't/hasn't + past participle*** ➜ **Fragen** mit ***have/has + past participle***
Signal-wörter	➜ *yesterday, last week/month/year, ago, in 2001, the other day*	➜ *already, recently, up to now, just, ever, yet, not yet, for, since*

SIMPLE PAST OR PRESENT PERFECT

1. Copy the text below into your exercise book.

a) Underline the signal words for the simple past in blue.

b) Underline the signal words for the present perfect in green.

c) Fill in the correct form of the simple past or the present perfect!

Amy and Rebecca ________________ (go) swimming yesterday. They ________________ (decide) to go to the indoor pool because it ________________ (be) cold and rainy outside. Amy ________________ (open) her bag last night when they ________________ (get) home because she ________________ (want) to take out her swimsuit. She ________________ (see) that her swimsuit was missing. She ________________ (buy) it recently. Amy ________________ just ________________ (call) the information desk of the indoor pool, but they ________________ (not find) her swimsuit yet. Amy is very sad, but then her mobile phone rings. It is the information desk. They tell her that they ________________ just ________________ (find) her swimsuit. Amy ________________ (not call) Rebecca yet to tell her the story, but she will soon.

EXPLANATION: SIMPLE PAST OR PAST PERFECT

Wenn **mehr als eine Zeitform** Anwendung findet, sollte man den **Inhalt** des Textes genau verstehen und mithilfe von **Signalwörtern** entscheiden, welche Zeitform angewandt werden soll.

	simple past	***past perfect***
Wann?	➜ **abgeschlossene** Ereignisse aus der Vergangenheit (Geschichten / Informationen)	➜ Ereignisse, die **vor einem abgeschlossenen Ereignis** in der Vergangenheit stattfanden
Wie?	➜ regelmäßige Verben: ***infinitive + ed*** ➜ unregelmäßige Verben: **müssen auswendig gelernt werden** ➜ **Verneinungen** mit dem Hilfsverb ***didn't*** ➜ **Fragen** mit dem Hilfsverb ***did***	➜ ***had + past participle*** ➜ **Verneinungen** mit ***hadn't + past participle*** ➜ **Fragen** mit ***had + past participle***
Signalwörter	➜ *yesterday, last week / month / year, ago, in 2001, the other day*	➜ *when, before, after, never, once, as soon as*

SIMPLE PAST OR PAST PERFECT

1. Copy the text below into your exercise book.

a) Underline the signal words for the simple past in blue.

b) Underline the signal words for the past perfect in green.

c) Fill in the correct form of the simple past or the past perfect!

John and Amy ________________ (meet) the other day because they ________________ (want) to plan a birthday party for Rebecca. Before they ________________ (meet) at John's house, they ________________ (talk) on the phone. John ________________ (tell) Amy that he ________________ already ________________ (plan) some surprise parties before. Amy ________________ (be) surprised because she ________________ never ________________ (hear) of that. Amy ________________ (go) to a decoration shop last week to get ideas for the party. She ________________ (not be) there before, and she ________________ (like) it very much. John ________________ (be) excited when he ________________ (hear) that Amy ________________ (think) about the party so much. That ________________ (be) the moment when he ________________ (know) that the party was going to be great. After John and Amy ________________ (meet), they ________________ (go) shopping together. They ________________ (organise) an unforgettable birthday party for Rebecca. She ________________ (enjoy) it a lot.

EXPLANATION: PRESENT PERFECT OR PRESENT PERFECT PROGRESSIVE

Wenn **mehr als eine Zeitform** Anwendung findet, sollte man den **Inhalt** des Textes genau verstehen und mithilfe von **Signalwörtern** entscheiden, welche Zeitform angewandt werden soll.

	present perfect	***present perfect progressive***
Wann?	➜ Ereignisse, die in der **Vergangenheit abgeschlossen** wurden, deren **Folgen** aber bis in die Gegenwart reichen ➜ **bis jetzt andauernde** Ereignisse aus der Vergangenheit ➜ **gerade beendete** Handlungen	➜ **bis jetzt andauernde** Ereignisse oder Handlungen aus der Vergangenheit ➜ Ereignisse oder Handlungen aus der Vergangenheit, die **kurz vorher endeten** ➜ Ereignisse, die über einen **bestimmten Zeitraum** hinweg stattfinden ➜ Betonung der **Dauer**
Wie?	➜ ***have/has + past participle*** ➜ **Verneinungen** mit ***haven't/hasn't + past participle*** ➜ **Fragen** mit ***have/has + past participle***	➜ ***have/has + been + ing form*** ➜ **Verneinungen** mit ***haven't/hasn't + been + ing form*** ➜ **Fragen** mit ***have/has + been + ing form***
Signal-wörter	➜ *already, recently, never, up to now, just, ever, yet, not yet, for, since*	➜ *since, for, all day/week/month*

PRESENT PERFECT OR PRESENT PERFECT PROGRESSIVE

1. Copy the text below into your exercise book.

a) Underline the signal words for the present perfect in blue.
b) Underline the signal words for the present perfect progressive in green.
c) Fill in the correct form of the present perfect or the present perfect progressive!

Rebecca ________________ (work) in the deli since 2018. Her best friend Amy ________________ just ________________ (finish) her studies and ________________ (start) to work there recently. Last week Rebecca broke her arm, so Amy is covering her shift in the deli. She ________________ (wash) dishes for three hours now. On top of that she ________________ (talk) to customers all day. She ________________ (not clean) the restrooms yet and is already very tired. However, she ________________ already ________________ (prepare) all the tables for the guests. She ________________ never ________________ (do) all these things on her own. Up to now she ________________ (share) all the work with Rebecca. She hopes that Rebecca will be better soon because she ________________ (work) very hard all week.

EXPLANATION: WILL-FUTURE OR GOING TO-FUTURE

Wenn **mehr als eine Zeitform** Anwendung findet, sollte man den Inhalt des Textes genau verstehen. Da die **Signalwörter** bei diesen beiden Zeitformen gleich sind, entscheidet hier ausschließlich der **Inhalt** über die Wahl der korrekten Zeitform.

	will-future	***going to-future***
Wann?	➜ bei **spontanen Entscheidungen** ➜ bei **Vermutungen, allgemeine Vorhersagen, Versprechen, Hoffnungen**	➜ bei **festen Plänen** für die Zukunft ➜ bei **absehbaren Ereignissen**, die in der Zukunft eintreffen werden
Wie?	➜ ***will + infinitive*** ➜ **Verneinungen** mit ***won't + infinitive*** ➜ **Fragen** mit ***will + infinitive***	➜ ***am/are/is + going to + infinitive*** ➜ **Verneinungen** mit ***am not/aren't/isn't + going to + infinitive*** ➜ **Fragen** mit ***am/are/is + going to + infinitive***
Signalwörter	➜ *tomorrow, soon, in the future, next week/month/year/Saturday/...*	➜ *tomorrow, soon, in the future, next week/month/year/Saturday/...*

WILL-FUTURE OR GOING TO-FUTURE

1. Copy the text below into your exercise book.
Fill in the correct form of the will-future or the going to-future!

Amy, Rebecca, Ben and Steven ________________ (meet) each other in the shopping centre in the afternoon. They ________________ (go) to the cinema together. Amy and Rebecca hope that they ________________ (not watch) a horror movie. They hope that it ________________ (be) a funny movie. Ben and Steven probably ________________ (not like) to watch a romantic movie. Rebecca has planned that she ________________ (eat) a lot of sweet popcorn. Amy ________________ (not have) sweet popcorn because she doesn't like it. But she probably ________________ (get) some crisps and a coke. The two boys have planned that they ________________ (buy) the extra-large special menu. It is a surprise menu, but the boys hope that they ________________ (get) a very big coke, a bucket full of popcorn and a bag full of crisps. There is one thing that the teens are sure of: They ________________ (have) a great time together.

EXPLANATION: ADJECTIVES AND ADVERBS

Adjectives (Adjektive) **beschreiben** Gegenstände und Personen, also **Nomen**.
Beispiel: *Rebecca has got an **old** car.*

Um nach einem *adjective* zu fragen, stellt man die Frage:
Wie ist etwas? / Wie ist jemand?

Adverbs (Adverbien) **beschreiben** genauer, wie etwas gemacht wird, und dienen somit der Beschreibung von **Verben**.
Beispiel: *Steven is running **quickly**, so that he can catch the bus.*

Um nach einem *adverb* zu fragen, stellt man die Frage:
Wie tut er/sie etwas? / Wie macht er/sie etwas?

Das ***adverb*** wird wie folgt gebildet: ***adjective + ly***

quick – quickly, happy – happily, funny – funnily

Beachte: Für *adjectives*, welche auf -ly enden, gibt es kein *adverb*.
friendly, lovely, unlikely, early, silly …

ACHTUNG

Unregelmäßige Formen:
good – well
long – long
short – short
little – little
fast – fast
early – early

Adjectives und *adverbs* können benutzt werden, um **Handlungen und Dinge miteinander zu vergleichen**.

ADJECTIVES AND ADVERBS

1. Copy the tables into your exercise book and fill in the missing forms.

1)

adjective	adverb
funny	
	quickly
early	
	well
fast	

2)

adjective	adverb
easy	
	loudly
	badly
slow	
short	

2. Adjective or adverb? Copy the sentences below and fill in the missing forms.

1) Steven and Ben can run ______________ (quick).

2) Rebecca is ______________ (happy) today.

3) Amy is ______________ (terrible) angry with her mother because she isn‘t allowed to go out.

4) Ben speaks to Amy ______________ (nice) to make her happy again.

5) Now Amy isn’t ______________ (angry) anymore.

EXPLANATION: COMPARISON OF ADJECTIVES AND ADVERBS

Für *adjectives* und *adverbs* gelten die **gleichen Steigerungsregeln**.
Es gibt immer **drei** Steigerungsformen:
1. *positive* (Positiv/Grundform), **2. *comparative*** (Komparativ), **3. *superlative*** (Superlativ)

Einsilbige *adjectives* und **zweisilbige** *adjectives*, die auf **-y, -er, -le** oder **-ow enden, werden mit -er und -est gesteigert**! **Einsilbige** *adverbs* und das *adverb* ***early*** werden **ebenfalls mit -er und -est gesteigert**.
*1. small – 2. small**er** – 3. the small**est**, 1. early – 2. earl**ier** – 3. the earl**iest***

Adjectives und *adverbs* mit **zwei oder mehr Silben** steigert man mit ***more*** und ***the most***.
*1. expensive – 2. **more** expensive – 3. **the most** expensive, 1. carefully – 2. **more** carefully – 3. **the most** carefully*

Wenn man **ungleiche Personen**, **Gegenstände** oder **Tiere** miteinander **vergleicht**, macht man das so:

comparative + than

Beispiel: *My brother runs **faster than** my best friend's brother.*

Wenn man zwei **gleiche Eigenschaften darstellt**, macht man das so:

as + positive + as

Beispiel: *Our class is **as funny as** the other class.*

ACHTUNG

Unregelmäßige Formen:
much – more – the most
bad/badly – worse – the worst
good/well – better – the best
little – less – the least

COMPARISON OF ADJECTIVES AND ADVERBS

1. Copy the adjectives and adverbs below.
a) Underline the adjectives in blue and the adverbs in red.
b) Write down the comparative and the superlative forms of the adjectives and adverbs.

1) funny	5) intelligent	9) well
2) carefully	6) pretty	10) quickly
3) happily	7) little	11) small
4) nasty	8) smart	12) badly

2. Translate the sentences into English and write them into your exercise book.

1) Meine Schwester ist so groß wie ich.
2) Der bellende Hund ist so laut wie mein Hund.
3) Englisch ist einfacher als Geschichte.
4) Deutsch ist am einfachsten.
5) Die Sommerferien sind am längsten.
6) Ich bin besser in Englisch als in Deutsch.

EXPLANATION: POSSESSIVE PRONOUNS

Possessive pronouns geben an, wem etwas **gehört**.
Im Englischen unterscheidet man zwischen dem ***possessive determiner*** (Possessivbegleiter) und dem ***possessive pronoun*** (Possessivpronomen).

➜ *Possessive determiners* **stehen vor dem Nomen.**
It isn't ***their*** *house.*

➜ *Possessive pronouns* **ersetzen ein Nomen** im Satz, also das Subjekt oder das Objekt des Satzes.
Their house is much bigger. ➜ ***Theirs*** *is much bigger.*

personal pronoun	*possessive determiner*	*possessive pronoun*
I	***my***	***mine***
you	***your***	***yours***
he	***his***	***his***
she	***her***	***hers***
it	***its***	***its***
we	***our***	***ours***
you	***your***	***yours***
they	***their***	***theirs***

POSSESSIVE PRONOUNS

1. Find the correct possessive pronouns to substitute the possessive determiners and the nouns. Write the sentences with the possessive pronouns into your exercise book.

1) Is this **your scarf**? ____________________
2) **Their car** is blue, not black. ____________________
3) That is **our dog**. ____________________
4) **Her scarf** is very colourful. ____________________
5) That is **my towel**. ____________________
6) The song we sang is **our song**. ____________________
7) **My class** is the coolest class in the world. ____________________
8) **Their new house** has got a red roof. ____________________
9) **My new leather jacket** is cool. ____________________
10) **Our school** has got the best teachers. ____________________
11) **Their homework** is as good as mine. ____________________

EXPLANATION: REFLEXIVE PRONOUNS

Reflexive pronouns (Reflexivpronomen) werden verwendet, wenn man ausdrücken möchte, dass jemand oder etwas **etwas selbst macht**. Sie **beziehen sich auf das Subjekt** des Satzes.

Beispiele: ***He** has fixed it **himself**.* ➔ *he* = Subjekt, *himself* = bezieht sich auf das Subjekt
***She** has cut **herself**.* ➔ *she* = Subjekt, *herself* = bezieht sich auf das Subjekt

So werden die *reflexive pronouns* gebildet:

subject	***reflexive pronoun***	***example***
I	***myself***	***I** have cut **myself**.*
you	***yourself***	***You** can do it **yourself**.*
he	***himself***	***Jim** has fixed the car **himself**.*
she	***herself***	***Nancy** has done the homework **herself**.*
it	***itself***	***It** has broken **itself**.*
we	***ourselves***	***We** have prepared **ourselves**.*
you	***yourselves***	***You** must work it out **yourselves**.*
they	***themselves***	***They** can do it **themselves**.*

REFLEXIVE PRONOUNS

1. Copy the sentences into your exercise book.
a) Underline the subjects of the sentences in red.
b) Fill in the missing reflexive pronouns.

1) My mom has prepared dinner ________________.
2) John's brother has made ________________ a sandwich.
3) The students have organised the class trip ________________.
4) The class has decorated the classroom ________________.
5) John, Marco and I are building a tree house ________________.
6) I have cut ________________ in the finger with the knife.
7) They have helped ________________ by working as a team.
8) She has never made jewellery ________________.
9) My friends and I will organise the summer holidays ________________.
10) You must all take the class test ________________.
11) John will repair the computer ________________.
12) The principal Mr Swang sometimes talks to ________________.
13) We didn't built the house ________________. It was built by a company.

EXPLANATION: RECIPROCAL PRONOUNS

Reciprocal pronouns (reziproke Pronomen) werden immer dann verwendet, wenn eine **Handlung zwischen zwei oder mehreren Personen stattfindet**.

Beispiele: *We have talked to **each other** every day.*
*They have called **one another** often.*

Anders als bei *reflexive pronouns* wird eine **Interaktion zwischen zwei oder mehreren Personen** deutlich.

➜ Im Englischen wird immer zwischen der wechselseitigen Aktion zwischen zwei Personen oder Gruppen (*reciprocal pronoun*) oder einer reflexiven Handlung (*reflexive pronoun*), welche nicht wechselseitig ist, unterschieden. Im Deutschen steht in beiden Fällen „sich".
*They look at **each other**.* – Sie schauen sich (gegenseitig) an.
*They look at **themselves**.* – Sie schauen sich (selbst) an.

Die *reciprocal pronouns* ***each other*** und ***one another*** haben die **gleiche Bedeutung**.

Beispiele: *We can meet **each other** in the city centre.*
*We can meet **one another** in the city centre.*

RECIPROCAL PRONOUNS

1. Copy the sentences into your exercise book.
a) Underline the subjects of the sentences in red.
b) Fill in the missing reciprocal pronouns or reflexive pronouns.

1) John and Marco write messages to ________________ every day.
2) Rebecca has cut ________________ in the finger.
3) Amy and Brian fell in love with ________________.
4) The students helped ________________ in the school project.
5) The girl made ________________ a sandwich.
6) My family and I planned the summer trip ________________.
7) My mom and dad played a card game with ________________ and my mom lost it.
8) We are going to see ________________ next week.
9) Marco has fixed his bike ________________.
10) Amy and Rebecca are going to see ________________ in the deli next week.
11) Amy has organised ________________ a job there.
12) Amy's sister and brother are going to paint the living room ________________.
13) John and Amy sometimes have dinner with ________________.

EXPLANATION: RELATIVE CLAUSES – WHO, WHICH, THAT

Ein ***relative clause*** (Relativsatz) wird verwendet, um **Gegenstände**, **Personen** oder **Tiere**, über die man spricht, **näher zu beschreiben**.

Relative clauses werden durch ***relative pronouns*** **eingeleitet**.
Es gibt unterschiedliche *relative pronouns*:

➜ ***Who*** wird verwendet, wenn man Personen näher beschreibt.
This is ***the girl who*** *always uses the bus.*
The kid who *never sleeps alone won't go on the class trip.*

➜ ***Which*** wird verwendet, wenn man Gegenstände oder Tiere näher beschreibt.
The shirt which *I love a lot is green.*
This is ***the dog which*** *is always friendly.*

➜ ***That*** kann für die Beschreibung von Tieren, Gegenständen und Personen verwendet werden.
The boy that *always plays football is my neighbour.*
The house that *has got a grey roof is very nice.*

RELATIVE CLAUSES – WHO, WHICH, THAT

1. Copy the sentences below into your exercise book and add the correct pronouns. Choose between who and which.

1) My mother is the woman ______________ I love the most.
2) My brother is the boy ______________ is wearing the blue shirt.
3) The car ______________ had an accident yesterday is standing over there.
4) The vacation ______________ we went on last summer was great.
5) The present ______________ I got for Christmas was the biggest.
6) The house ______________ is pink can be found in Los Angeles.
7) The children ______________ live next door are very nice.
8) The dog ______________ barks is cute.
9) My classmate ______________ is always late didn't catch the bus yesterday.
10) The students ______________ have got a small classroom talked to the principal.

2. Copy the sentences into your exercise book and finish them. Use relative pronouns.

1) My best friend ____.
2) The house ____.

EXPLANATION: RELATIVE CLAUSES – WHOSE, WHOM

Ein ***relative clause*** (Relativsatz) wird verwendet, um **Gegenstände**, **Personen** oder **Tiere**, über welche man spricht, **näher zu beschreiben**.

Relative clauses werden durch ***relative pronouns*** **eingeleitet**.
Es gibt unterschiedliche *relative pronouns*:

➜ ***Whose*** wird verwendet, wenn man anzeigen möchte, wem etwas gehört oder zu wem etwas gehört.
*The woman **whose car** is red lives next to me.*
*The class **whose teacher** is always ill is going to get a new teacher.*

➜ ***Whom*** wird verwendet, um das Objekt des Satzes näher zu beschreiben.
Das Objekt muss eine Person sein.
*In my school we have **a teacher whom** we all like.*
*That is **the student whom** we interviewed last month.*

ACHTUNG

Direkt hinter dem *relative pronoun* **whom** darf **kein Verb** stehen.

RELATIVE CLAUSES – WHOSE, WHOM

1. Connect the sentences by using the relative pronouns whose and whom.
Write the connected sentences into your exercise book.
Be careful. Some sentences change their structure.

1) This is the nice boy. I met him last week.
2) That is Lucy. Her house is big.
3) There are many animals in the neighbourhood. I know their owners.
4) That is Jack. I have known him since I was a baby.
5) There are many children here. Their parents are at work.
6) Rebecca visits her friend Jamie. Jamie's brother lives in Germany.
7) This is my friend Steven. I have liked him from the beginning.
8) That is the Barker family. My siblings meet them every Sunday.
9) This is Melissa. Her parents come from Ireland.
10) Over there are many Native Americans. I have read a lot about them.
11) These are my best friends Amy and Rebecca. Their dream is to work as teachers.

EXPLANATION: IF-CLAUSES – TYPE I

If-clauses I sind **Bedingungssätze**. Man kann sie auch als „**Wenn…, dann… -Sätze**“ bezeichnen.
➜ Bei *if-clauses* des **Typ I**, ist es **sehr wahrscheinlich**, **dass das Ereignis eintreten wird**.

So bildet man einen *if-clause* Typ I:

*If I **go** to London,*	*I **will visit** the London Eye.*
simple present (im *if-clause*)	***will-future*** (im Hauptsatz)
infinitive oder ***he, she, it*** **– das -s muss mit**	***will + infinitive***

Beispiele: *Her mom **will be** mad if she **comes** home late.*
*If I **don't travel** to New York, I **won't go** shopping.*

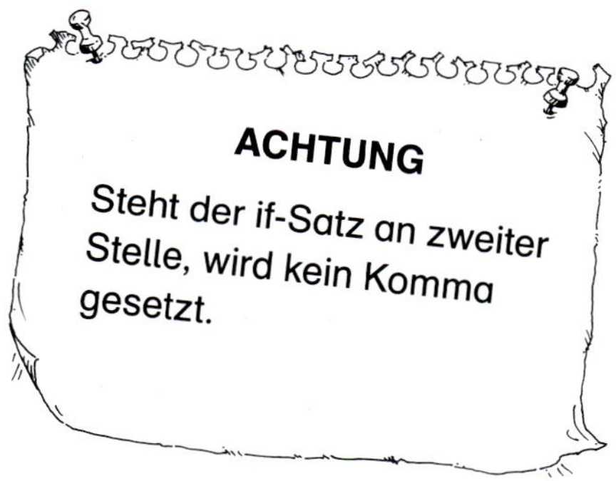

IF-CLAUSES – TYPE I

1. Copy the sentences below into your exercise book. Put in the correct tense. Use if-clauses type I.

1) If Rebecca and John ________________ (visit) their grandma, she ________________ (cook) them their favourite dish.

2) John ________________ (get) a good mark if he ________________ (study) for the maths test.

3) John and Marco ________________ (have) fun if they ________________ (go) to the park together.

4) If Rebecca ________________ (not work) in the deli, she ________________ (not have) enough money for her trip to California next summer.

5) If the sun ________________ (shine) tomorrow, Amy and Rebecca ________________ (eat) some ice cream at the park.

6) Rebecca's boss ________________ (be) mad if she ________________ (come) late for work.

7) Marco ________________ (become) a fire fighter if he ________________ (have) good grades in school.

8) John ________________ (go) to New York next summer if his mom ________________ (allow) the trip.

9) If Rebecca ________________ (work) hard in the deli, she ________________ (get) more money.

10) John and Marco ________________ (not go) swimming if it ________________ (rain).

2. Form five if-clauses type I and write them into your exercise book. Use the correct tenses.

EXPLANATION: IF-CLAUSES – TYPE II

If clauses II sind **Bedingungssätze**. Man kann sie auch als „**Was wäre, wenn ...-Sätze**“ bezeichnen.
➜ Bei *if-clauses* des **Typ II** ist es **eher unwahrscheinlich**, **dass die Bedingung eintritt**.

So bildet man einen *if-clause* Typ II:

*If I **had** much money,*	*I **would buy** a lot of clothes.*
simple past (im *if-clause*)	***conditional I*** (im Hauptsatz)
infinitive + ed oder **unregelmäßige Verbform**	***would + infinitive***

Beispiele: *If the schools **didn't close** during the summer, I **would have** to study a lot.*
*If my friends **went** to Spain with me, we **would have** a lot of fun.*

ACHTUNG

Steht der if-Satz an zweiter Stelle, wird kein Komma gesetzt.

IF-CLAUSES – TYPE II

1. Copy the sentences below into your exercise book. Put in the correct tense. Use if-clauses type II.

1) If John ________________ (have) $1000, he ________________ (buy) a lot of clothes.
2) Marco ________________ (go) hiking in the summer if it ________________ (not be) too hot.
3) If Rebecca ________________ (win) the lottery, she ________________ (buy) herself a new car.
4) Amy ________________ (be) happy if she and Rebecca ________________ (go) to Disney World together.
5) If the class ________________ (do) the homework, they ________________ (get) a good oral mark.
6) Rebecca ________________ (not work) in the deli if she ________________ (have) a lot of money.
7) Amy ________________ (be) happy if she ________________ (have) a dog.
8) John and Marco ________________ (be) in big trouble if they ________________ (come) late for class.
9) Rebecca ________________ (be) excited if she ________________ (win) a shopping trip.
10) If Amy ________________ (turn) 21 next week, she ________________ (have) a great party.
11) Marco ________________ (have) a pool party if he ________________ (have) a big pool.

2. Form five if-clauses type II and write them into your exercise book. Use the correct tenses.

EXPLANATION: IF-CLAUSES – TYPE III

If clauses III sind **Bedingungssätze**. Man kann sie auch als „**Was wäre gewesen, wenn …-Sätze**“ bezeichnen.
➜ Es ist **unmöglich**, **dass die Bedingung des Typ III eintritt**, da sie sich **auf** die **Vergangenheit bezieht**.

So bildet man einen *if-clause* Typ III:

*If I **had found** the map,*	*I **would have found** the way home.*
past perfect (im *if-clause*)	***conditional II*** (im Hauptsatz)
had + past participle	***would + have + past participle***

Beispiele: *If the summer **hadn't been** that hot, we **would have gone** hiking more often.*
*If the trip **had been** longer, we **would have visited** my aunt Sara.*
*The day **wouldn't have been** that great if it **had rained**.*

ACHTUNG

Steht der if-Satz an zweiter Stelle, wird kein Komma gesetzt.

IF-CLAUSES – TYPE III

PARTS OF SPEECH

1. Copy the sentences below into your exercise book. Put in the correct tense. Use if-clauses type III.

1) If the weather ________________ (not be) so nice, we ________________ (not go) swimming.

2) If John and Marco ________________ (not miss) the bus, they ________________ (be) in school on time.

3) The girls ________________ (go) to the park if the weather ________________ (be) fine.

4) Marco ________________ (get) better grades if he ________________ (study) more for the tests.

5) If the entrance fee ________________ (be) too high, Marco and John ________________ (not go) to the zoo.

6) If Rebecca ________________ (not work) a lot, she ________________ (not go) on the great round trip.

7) If Marco ________________ (not go) to the cinema last week, he ________________ (not meet) his new girlfriend Sue.

8) Marco ________________ (visit) his aunt last month if the flight ________________ (not be) cancelled.

2. Form five if-clauses type III and write them into your exercise book. Use the correct tenses.

EXPLANATION: ACTIVE AND PASSIVE VOICE

Mithilfe der ***active voice*** und der ***passive voice*** kann man bestimmen, welcher **Teil eines Satzes betont werden** soll.

Mit der *active voice* betont man, **wer oder was etwas macht** (Subjekt).

Beispiel: *My mom* ***cooked*** *dinner. (active voice in the simple past)*

Mit der *passive voice* betont man, **was getan wird** (Verb).

➜ Die *passive voice* setzt sich grundsätzlich immer aus **zwei Teilen** zusammen:

form of (to) be + past participle

Beispiel: *Dinner* ***was cooked*** *by my mom. (passive voice in the simple past)*

Wenn man einen Satz in der *passive voice* bildet, wird das **Objekt des Aktivsatzes zum Subjekt des Passivsatzes**.

➜ Um in der *passive voice* zu sagen, **wer eine Handlung ausgeführt hat**, nutzt man den ***by-agent***.
The house ***was cleaned by*** *my brother.*

➜ Auch **ohne *by-agent*** ist ein Satz in der *passive voice* vollständig.
The house ***was cleaned***.

ACTIVE AND PASSIVE VOICE

1. Answer the questions in German. Write the answers into your exercise book.

1) When do you use the active voice?
2) When do you use the passive voice?

2. Are the sentences written in the active voice or the passive voice? Write the answers into your exercise book.

1) The house was built by the workers. ____________________
2) The workers built the house. ____________________
3) My dad puts up the tent. ____________________
4) The tent is put up by my dad. ____________________
5) I have cleaned my room. ____________________
6) My room has been cleaned. ____________________
7) Rebecca drove the car. ____________________
8) The car was driven by Rebecca. ____________________
9) The song is sung by my family. ____________________
10) My family sings the song. ____________________

EXPLANATION: ACTIVE AND PASSIVE IN THE SIMPLE PRESENT

In der ***active voice*** gilt für das ***simple present*** die Regel:

***he, she, it* – das -s muss mit!**

Beispiele: *The kids **love** their cat.*
*Amy **loves** her cat.*

Mit den Hilfsverben ***do/does*** werden **Fragen** im *simple present* formuliert.

Beispiele: ***Do** the kids love their cat?*
***Does** Amy love her cat?*

Mit den Hilfsverben ***don't/doesn't*** werden **Verneinungen** im *simple present* gebildet.

Beispiele: *The kids **don't love** their cat.*
*Amy **doesn't love** her cat.*

Die ***passive voice*** im ***simple present*** wird wie folgt gebildet:

am/are/is + past participle

Beachte: *I am, you are, he/she/it is, we are, you are, they are*

Beispiele: *The cat **is loved** by Amy.*
***Is** the cat **loved** by Amy?*
*The cat **isn't loved** by Amy.*

ACTIVE AND PASSIVE IN THE SIMPLE PRESENT

1. Copy the sentences below into your exercise book.
a) Underline the subjects in red, the objects in blue and the verbs in green.
b) Put the sentences into the passive voice and write them into your exercise book.

1) The children love the teacher.
2) My dog plays with the ball.
3) Marco cleans his room.
4) John does the English homework.
5) The boys kick the ball.

2. Copy the sentences below into your exercise book.
a) Underline the subjects in red, the objects in blue and the verbs in green.
b) Put the sentences into the active voice and write them into your exercise book.

1) The house is kept clean by my mom.
2) The horses are fed by my sister.
3) My dog is played with by me.
4) The garage is painted by my family.
5) The bike is fixed by me.

EXPLANATION: ACTIVE AND PASSIVE IN THE SIMPLE PAST

In der ***active voice*** gilt für das ***simple past*** die Regel:

infinitive + ed oder unregelmäßige _simple past_ Verbform (bei unregelmäßigen Verben)

Beispiele: *John **kicked** the ball.*
*The children **spoke** to Amy.*

Mit dem Hilfsverb ***did*** werden **Fragen** im *simple past* formuliert.
Beispiel: ***Did** John kick the ball?*

Mit dem Hilfsverb ***didn't*** werden **Verneinungen** im *simple past* gebildet.
Beispiel: *John **didn't** kick the ball.*

Die ***passive voice*** im ***simple past*** wird wie folgt gebildet:

was/were + past participle

Beachte: *I was, you were, he/she/it was, we were, you were, they were*

Beispiele: *The bike **was fixed** by Marco./The bikes **were fixed** by Marco.*
***Was** the bike **fixed** by Marco?/**Were** the bikes **fixed** by Marco?*
*The bike **wasn't fixed** by Marco./The bikes **weren't fixed** by Marco.*

ACTIVE AND PASSIVE IN THE SIMPLE PAST

1. Copy the sentences below into your exercise book.
a) Underline the subjects in red, the objects in blue and the verbs in green.
b) Put the sentences into the passive voice and write them into your exercise book.

1) Rebecca drove the car.
2) Amy carried the basket.
3) Someone cleaned the kitchen.
4) My brother ate the cookies.
5) I did my homework.

2. Copy the sentences below into your exercise book.
a) Underline the subjects in red, the objects in blue and the verbs in green.
b) Put the sentences into the active voice and write them into your exercise book.

1) The houses were destroyed by the storm.
2) The queen was taken to her palace by a helicopter.
3) The mess was made by the children.
4) The guests were entertained by the clown.
5) The grandmother was visited by her grandchildren.

EXPLANATION: ACTIVE AND PASSIVE IN THE PRESENT PERFECT

In der ***active voice*** gilt für das ***present perfect*** die Regel:

have/has + past participle

Beachte: *I have, you have, he/she/it has, we have, you have, they have*

Beispiele: *John **has kicked** the ball.*
*The children **have spoken** to Amy.*

Fragen werden ebenfalls mit ***have/has + past participle*** gebildet.

Beispiel: ***Has** John **kicked** the ball?*

Verneinungen werden mit ***have/has + not + past participle*** gebildet.

Beispiel: *John **hasn't kicked** the ball.*

Die ***passive voice*** im ***present perfect*** wird wie folgt gebildet:

have/has + been + past participle

Beachte: *I have, you have, he/she/it has, we have, you have, they have*

Beispiele: *The bike **has been fixed** by Marco./The bikes **have been fixed** by Marco.*
***Has** the bike **been fixed** by Marco?/**Have** the bikes **been fixed** by Marco?*
*The bike **hasn't been fixed** by Marco./The bikes **haven't been fixed** by Marco.*

ACTIVE AND PASSIVE IN THE PRESENT PERFECT

1. Copy the sentences below into your exercise book.
a) Underline the subjects in red, the objects in blue and the verbs in green.
b) Put the sentences into the passive voice and write them into your exercise book.

1) My brother has cleaned the garage.
2) Our uncle has paid for the holiday.
3) The children have prepared the meal.
4) No one has seen the dog all day.
5) My teacher has corrected the homework.

2. Copy the sentences below into your exercise book.
a) Underline the subjects in red, the objects in blue and the verbs in green.
b) Put the sentences into the active voice and write them into your exercise book.

1) The bags have been carried by the students.
2) The church has been designed by a famous architect.
3) The elephant has been fed by the zookeeper.
4) The goods have been produced by the company.
5) The roof has been fixed by our dad.

EXPLANATION: ACTIVE AND PASSIVE IN THE PAST PERFECT

In der ***active voice*** gilt für das ***past perfect*** die Regel:

had + past participle

Beispiele: *John **had kicked** the ball.*
*The children **had spoken** to Amy.*

Fragen werden ebenfalls mit ***had + past participle*** gebildet.
Beispiel: ***Had** John **kicked** the ball?*

Verneinungen werden mit ***had + not + past participle*** gebildet.
Beispiel: *John **hadn't kicked** the ball.*

Die ***passive voice*** im ***past perfect*** wird wie folgt gebildet:

had + been + past participle

Beispiele: *The bike **had been fixed** by Marco. / The bikes **had been fixed** by Marco.*
***Had** the bike **been fixed** by Marco? / **Had** the bikes **been fixed** by Marco?*
*The bike **hadn't been fixed** by Marco. / The bikes **hadn't been fixed** by Marco.*

ACTIVE AND PASSIVE IN THE PAST PERFECT

1. Copy the sentences below into your exercise book.
a) Underline the subjects in red, the objects in blue and the verbs in green.
b) Put the sentences into the passive voice and write them into your exercise book.

1) Marco had done his homework.
2) The workers had built the house.
3) Picasso had painted the painting.
4) Amy had picked up her driver's licence.
5) The tailor had designed a new dress.

2. Copy the sentences below into your exercise book.
a) Underline the subjects in red, the objects in blue and the verbs in green.
b) Put the sentences into the active voice and write them into your exercise book.

1) The book had been written by a famous author.
2) The dish had been cooked by John.
3) The monkeys had been fed by the visitors.
4) The farm had been renovated by the farmer.
5) The roof had been fixed by my dad.

EXPLANATION: GERUND AS A SUBJECT

Im Englischen können **Verben**, wie auch im Deutschen, **nominalisiert werden**.

➜ Ein **nominalisiertes Verb** nennt man im Englischen ***gerund***.
➜ Das *gerund* ist auch als **ing-Form des Verbs** bekannt.
➜ Nominalisierung bedeutet, dass ein **Verb zu einem Nomen umgewandelt wird**.
*Do not **park** on the road. ➔ **Parking** on the road isn't allowed.*

Das *gerund* kann **als Subjekt** des Satzes verwendet werden und steht dann am **Satzanfang**.

Beispiele: ***Singing** songs together is great.*
***Dancing** makes me happy.*

GERUND AS A SUBJECT

1. Copy the sentences below and fill in the gaps with the gerund.

1) ____________ (watch) a good movie is something I love to do.
2) ____________ (ride) in the woods is a great feeling.
3) ____________ (meet) my friends is never boring.
4) ____________ (ask) someone for help is a good thing to do.
5) ____________ (play) football is my favourite hobby.
6) ____________ (enjoy) the sunset is something Rebecca loves very much.

2. Form sentences and write them into your exercise book.

1) . – your bike – fixing – tricky – can be
2) on the computer – . – can hurt – working – your eyes
3) playing – on the street – . – with your mobile phone – is dangerous
4) a picknick – is awesome – having – . – in the park – with friends
5) outside – playing – is a lot of fun – . – with friends

EXPLANATION: GERUND AS AN OBJECT

Das *gerund* kann im Englischen nicht nur als Subjekt dienen, sondern **auch als Objekt verwendet werden**.

Beispiele: *I love **watching** tv at night.*
*I don't like **studying** for tests.*

Das *gerund* **als Objekt** benutzt man fast immer, wenn man **ausdrückt**, **was man mag oder nicht mag**.

Beispiele: *I enjoy **meeting** my friends.*
*I don't like **waiting** for someone.*

Das *gerund* **als Objekt** steht häufig **hinter diesen Verben**:
like, enjoy, love, prefer, start, stop, hate, suggest, miss, keep, risk, finish

Beispiele: *Eva enjoys **spending** time with her family.*
*Nina likes **watching** animated movies.*
*Chris prefers **watching** science fiction.*
*Felix keeps **jumping** on the trampoline.*
*Nele starts **singing** "We will rock you".*

GERUND AS AN OBJECT

1. Copy the sentences below and fill in the gaps with the gerund.

1) Roland can't stop ________________ (play) his favourite computer game.
2) Luca keeps ________________ (practice) for his driver's licence test.
3) Ute enjoys ________________ (cook) for the whole family.
4) Amy doesn't like ________________ (eat) alone.
5) The dog has just stopped ________________ (chase) after the ball.

2. Form sentences and write them into your exercise book.

1) drinking – I – . – have never liked – energy drinks
2) . – love – around Italy – the students – travelling
3) to the radio – kept – the children – . – listening
4) Christmas – my family – celebrating – . – likes – in Austria
5) stopped – last night – the car – . – working
6) they – . – watching – in the cinema – suggested – the new movie

EXPLANATION: GERUND AFTER A PREPOSITION

PARTS OF SPEECH

Wenn das **Verb direkt hinter einer *preposition*** (Präposition) steht, **muss das *gerund* gebildet werden**.

➜ *Prepositions* sind Worte wie:
***to**, **by**, **for**, **before**, **of**, **after**, **about**, **at**, **in**, **on** …*

➜ *Prepositions* drücken räumliche, zeitliche und sonstige Beziehungen aus.

➜ *Prepositions* können vor *gerunds* stehen.

Beispiele: *She is good **at singing**.*
*They are excited **about going** on vacation.*
*I am scared **of seeing** a ghost.*

Im Englischen gibt es **Wortzusammensetzungen** aus Verben und Adverben, welche man als ***phrasal verbs*** bezeichnet.

➜ Am Ende mancher *phrasal verbs* steht ein „***to***“, welches als *preposition* fungiert.
*I **look forward to seeing** you next summer.*

GERUND AFTER A PREPOSITION

1. Copy the sentences into your exercise book.
a) Add the gerunds to the sentences and put them in the right place.
b) Underline the prepositions.

1) She – is looking forward to – her best friend – next weekend. (meet)
2) Nele – is excited about – a kitten. (get)
3) The kids – are used to – their homework – after school. (do)
4) Felix – is interested in – books – about technology. (read)
5) She – will go – home – after – the movie. (watch)
6) Luca – has – always – dreamed of – a – youtuber. (be)
7) My mom – is – worried about – ill. (get)
8) Amy's brother – is tired of – late at school. (stay)
9) Eva – is good at – animals. (help)
10) Ute – has always dreamed of – in the USA. (live)
11) Clemens – is famous for – sports – every day. (do)
12) Many singers – are proud of – a great voice. (have)
13) The British – are famous for – their afternoon tea. (drink)

EXPLANATION: MODAL AUXILIARIES

Modal auxiliaries werden verwendet, um auszudrücken, ob eine **Handlung durchgeführt werden muss, kann, darf oder soll**.

➜ Häufig verwendete *modal auxiliaries* sind:
can **(können),** ***must*** **(müssen),** ***may*** **(dürfen),** ***shall*** **(sollen),** ***will*** **(würden),** ***could*** **(könnten),** ***might*** **(könnten),** ***should*** **(sollten),** ***would*** **(würden)**

➜ Auf ein *modal auxiliary* folgt immer ein Infinitiv.
They ***may go*** *to the party next weekend.*

Um einzelne *modal auxiliaries* in allen Zeitformen verwenden zu können, gibt es **Ersatzformen**:

can → to be able to
She ***can*** *sing./She* ***was able to*** *sing./She* ***has been able to*** *sing./…*

must → have to
She ***must*** *go home./She* ***had to*** *go home./She* ***has had to*** *go home./…*

may → to be allowed to
Amy ***may*** *go out./Amy* ***was allowed to*** *go out./Amy* ***has been allowed to*** *go out./…*

MODAL AUXILIARIES

1. Copy the sentences below into your exercise book.
a) Underline the modal auxiliaries in the sentences.
b) Rewrite the sentences into your exercise book by using the substitute form *(Ersatzform)* and the tense in the brackets.

1) Marco can play football every day. (simple past)
2) Amy may work in the deli. (will-future)
3) Rebecca must work in the deli. (simple past)
4) John must study. (simple present)
5) Clemens may travel the world. (present perfect)
6) Luca can drive any car. (present perfect)
7) Chris must help his mom. (simple past)
8) Marco must go home. (simple present)
9) Mary can visit her friend in Wales. (present perfect)
10) John can watch a movie. (simple present)
11) Amy may fly to Spain. (simple past)

Bevor man einen Text liest, sollte man immer überlegen, worum es in dem Text gehen könnte.

➜ Meist befinden sich neben den Lesetexten **Bilder** und **Illustrationen**. Diese können **erste Hinweise** auf den **Inhalt** des Textes geben.
➜ Auch die ***headings*** (Überschriften) zeigen meist an, um was es in dem Text geht.

Beispiele:

Heading and picture 1:
"A daytrip to the zoo"

ideas: family visits the zoo, animals, elephant, tiger, sunny, rainy, class trip, friends, fun, exciting, boring

Heading and picture 2:
"Christmas shopping in New York – people go crazy"

ideas: Christmas, mall/shopping centre, gift/present, many people, Santa Clause, kids, spending money, a lot of people want to buy the same things

PRE-READING ACTIVITY – THE HEADING AND THE PICTURE

1. Match the headings and the picture with the correct texts. Write the number of the text and the heading/the picture into your exercise book.

1) The students are celebrating. They have finally got their long-expected new sports field, which they have been fighting for for the last five years.

2) It looks a little bit like some sort of slime and if you don't know it, you might not like it. But in most parts of Scotland it is a typical breakfast dish which is usually served with fruit. It is called porridge.

3) The Miller family is still shocked. They went swimming at the greatest beach in Florida. Suddenly the emergency bells rang, after a group of sharks attacked a crowd of fish in the sea.

A typical Scottish breakfast

New sports field at Rossview High

2. What could the texts be about? Write your ideas into your exercise book.

A year abroad

A daytrip to New York City

EXPLANATION: SKIMMING

Das ***skimming*** ist eine **Lesestrategie**, …

➜ welche man meistens anwendet, wenn man an einem **neuen Text arbeitet**.
➜ die auch als **orientierendes Lesen** bezeichnet wird.
➜ bei der man den Text **überfliegt**, um sich einen **groben Überblick** zu verschaffen.

Folgende **Informationen** kann man mithilfe von *skimming* einem Text entnehmen:

1) Um welche **Textart** handelt es sich?
Brief, Postkarte, Geschichte, Informationstext …

2) Welche **Charaktere** werden in dem Text angesprochen?
Um wen geht es in der Geschichte, für wen ist der Brief …

3) Welche **Handlung** oder **Schlüsselinformationen** kann man dem Text entnehmen? Gibt es **Schlüsselwörter**, die auf den Inhalt hinweisen?

ACHTUNG

Beim *skimming* liest man nicht jedes Wort in einem Text, sondern überfliegt ihn nur!

1. a) What could the text be about? Create a mind map in your exercise book based on the heading and the picture.
b) Skim the text and write the keywords into your exercise book.
c) What is the text about? Write 2–3 sentences about it into your exercise book.

____

____

A trip around the British Isles

The British Isles are a well-known tourist destination. There is a great variety of activities, destinations, sights, and cultural events which are worth a visit.
Lovers of the Middle Ages like to visit the British Isles because of the ancient towns, old castles, and its history. Tourists enjoy travelling around the country very much. It is easy to get around because most of the famous tourist destinations are easy to reach by bus or by train. Stonehenge is one of the most mythical sights of the British Isles, and is located in the north of the city Salisbury. Stonehenge is one of the best-known prehistoric monuments. Another great place to visit is the city of London. Its cultural events and the great number of sights are worth seeing.

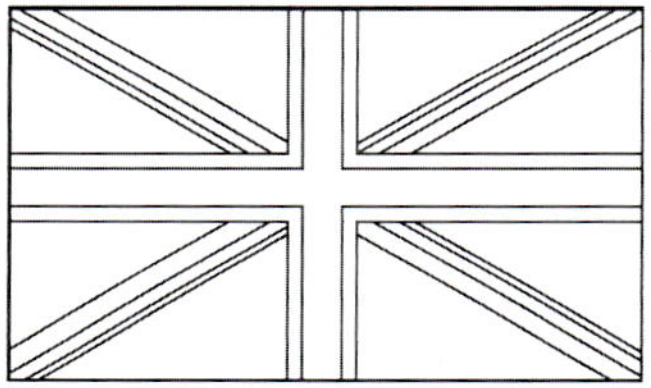

EXPLANATION: SCANNING

Das ***scanning*** ist eine **Lesestrategie**, …

- ➜ welche man meistens anwendet, wenn man nach **bestimmten Informationen** in einem Text sucht. Wie ein Scanner überfliegt man den Text mit seinen Augen.
- ➜ bei der man sich den Text nur **flüchtig** ansieht.
- ➜ bei der man den Text **nicht genau verstehen**, sondern nur die benötigten Informationen finden muss.

Man wendet die Lesetechnik *scanning* an, wenn man …

1) **Fragen** hat, die man zu dem Text **beantworten** soll.
2) nach einer **bestimmten Information** sucht.
3) nach **Namen oder Personen** sucht.
4) bestimmte **Begriffe** sucht.

ACHTUNG

Suche nach ***keywords*** (Schlüsselwörtern), wenn du bestimmte Informationen suchst!

SCANNING

1. Scan the text and answer the following questions. Write the answers into your exercise book.

1) Who was the first famous settler?
2) When did Columbus reach North America?
3) Where did most of the first settlers come from?
4) Why did some Europeans go to North America?
5) How many colonies did the British have by 1770?

In 1493 Columbus reached the so-called New World. Most of the first Europeans to reach North America came from Spain.
The inhabitants of Europe were interested to settle in North America to gain influence in the world. They wanted to gain more money and wealth, and they also tried to escape religious discrimination. In 1607 the first British colony was founded and named Jamestown. In 1620 a specific religious group named Pilgrims came to North America and founded another colony, which they named Plymouth. By 1770 the British had built up 13 colonies in North America, and about two million people lived and worked there. Enslaved Africans made up a great number of inhabitants there, and were forced to work for the Europeans.

EXPLANATION: DETAILED READING

Unter ***detailed reading*** versteht man das **genaue Lesen** eines Textes.

→ *Detailed reading* findet Anwendung, wenn man einen **komplizierten Artikel**, **Sach- oder Fachtext** liest, dessen Inhalt man verstehen muss.

Detailed reading bedeutet jedoch nicht, dass man jeden Satz langsam und mehrfach liest, sondern beinhaltet eine **Strategie**, wie man mit **unbekannten Wörtern** und **schwer verständlichen Textpassagen** umgeht.

Beim *detailed reading* wird Folgendes **markiert**:

1) unbekannte Wörter

2) schwer verständliche Textstellen

→ Unbekannte Wörter und Textstellen sollten **nur nachgeschlagen** werden, wenn sie für das **Textverständnis notwendig** sind.

ACHTUNG

Man wählt Symbole/Farben, mit welchen schwere Abschnitte und Wörter markiert werden können!

DETAILED READING

1. a) Read the text and write unknown words and difficult phrases into your exercise book.
b) Look up the words in a dictionary and write the translation next to the difficult words/phrases into your exercise book.
c) Read the text again and check if it is easier to understand the text now.

The head of the British Royal Family is the Queen. The Queen must take care of many state and national duties as she strengthens national unity. Throughout the year the Royal Family carries out over 2000 official engagements, which means that the Queen herself is not able to act as a representative at each event.
Therefore, the Queen is supported by her family, which is her son and grandchildren with their spouses.
The representation includes being present at official state events, charity events and visits to foreign countries to strengthen the economic and diplomatic relations of Great Britain. Additionally, the Royal Family hosts a great number of events every year. These events include lunches, garden parties and dinners at the Royal residences all over the world.

EXPLANATION: WRITING ABOUT YOUR HOLIDAY DESTINATION

WRITING

Wenn man über **Urlaubsziele** berichtet, können folgende Informationen in den Text integriert werden:

1) **Ort:** Wohin reist man?
2) **Zeit:** Wann findet die Reise statt?
3) **Dauer:** Wie lange verreist man?
4) **Aktivitäten:** Was kann man dort unternehmen?
5) **Begleitung:** Mit wem verreist man?

➜ Vor dem Schreiben sollte ein **Schreibplan** anhand der Leitfragen erstellt werden, damit man keine wichtigen Informationen vergisst.

Diese Aspekte sind beim Schreiben zu berücksichtigen:

1) Der Text sollte interessant gestaltet sein. Das erreicht man, indem man **Adjektive** verwendet.
2) Die Sätze sollten **kurz** und **gut verständlich** sein und einzelne Themen sollten in **Absätzen** organisiert werden.
3) Es sollten **Verbindungswörter** wie *and*, *but*, *because* usw. verwendet werden.
4) Man verwendet **Zukunftsformen** und das ***simple present***.

WRITING ABOUT YOUR HOLIDAY DESTINATION

1. Create a writing plan. Answer the questions. Write the answers into your exercise book.

1) Where are you going to travel?
2) When are you going to go there?
3) How long are you going to stay?
4) What can you do there? Are there any special activities?
5) Who is going to come with you?

2. a) Write a text about your holiday destination. Consider the aspects that are important while writing about your holiday destination.
b) Check your text. Have you considered the following aspects?

1) Have you used short and clear sentences?
2) Have you used adjectives to make it more interesting?
3) Have you used connectives like and, because, but …?
4) Have you used the future tenses and the simple present?

EXPLANATION: WRITING AN E-MAIL

Bevor man eine **E-Mail** schreibt, sollte man Folgendes bedenken:

1) Wer ist der **Empfänger** der Mail? Ein Freund (***informal mail***) oder eine fremde Person bzw. eine Respektsperson (***formal mail***)?

2) Wie lautet der **Betreff** (***subject***), also die Überschrift der Mail?

3) Wie **begrüßt** man den Empfänger angemessen?

informal mail	***formal mail***
Hi ...,/Hey ...,/Dear ...,/Hello ...,/...	*Dear Sir or Madam,/Dear Ladies and Gentlemen,/...*

4) Was möchte man dem Empfänger schreiben? Was ist der **Inhalt** der Mail?

5) Wie **verabschiedet** man sich angemessen?

informal mail	***formal mail***
Hope to see you soon./Bye!/Yours, .../Love, .../...	*Kind regards, .../Sincerely, .../Sincerely yours, .../...*

WRITING AN E-MAIL

1. Create a writing plan and answer the email.

to:	can103@germanmail.de
from:	joe.bolt@usmail.com
subject:	Visit me in the USA

Hello Can,

I hope that you are doing fine!? How have you been lately? When I visited you in Germany last year you said that you would like to visit my family and me in the USA this year. Is that still your plan? Where would you like to go? New York, California, Florida? I would love to show you all the places that you want to visit! Is there something special you would like to eat when you come here? My mom is a great cook!

I hope to hear from you soon!

Yours, Joe

EXPLANATION: WRITING A FORMAL AND AN INFORMAL LETTER

Bevor man einen **Brief** schreibt, sollte man Folgendes bedenken:

1) Wer ist der **Empfänger** des Briefs? Ein Freund (***informal letter***) oder eine fremde Person bzw. eine Respektsperson (***formal letter***)?

2) Wie lautet die **Adresse des Empfängers**?

3) Wie lautet das **Datum**?

4) Wie **begrüßt** man den Empfänger angemessen?

informal letter	***formal letter***
Hi …,/Hey …,/Dear …,/Hello …,/…	*Dear Sir or Madam,/Dear Ladies and Gentlemen,/…*

5) Was möchte man dem Empfänger schreiben? Was ist das **Anliegen**?

6) Wie **verabschiedet** man sich angemessen?

informal letter	***formal letter***
Hope to hear from you soon./Bye!/Yours, …/ Love, …/	*Kind regards, …/Yours faithfully, …/ Sincerely yours, …/…*

WRITING A FORMAL AND AN INFORMAL LETTER

1. The letter is messed up. Write down the letter in the correct order into your exercise book!

Sincerely yours, Danny Holt

12th October 2021

Computer Services J. & F.
Springfield Road 26
1489 California

Dear Ladies and Gentlemen,

Do you need me to send the broken computer back to you, or are the pictures enough for evidence? What steps should I take next?

I am sending this mail because I have ordered a new computer in your shop. It was sent to me and as you can see in the picture the screen is broken.

2. Write a letter to your friend and tell him/her what you did last weekend. Don't forget to create a writing plan first.

EXPLANATION: WRITING A REPORT

Ein ***report*** ist ein **Bericht**, der folgende Fragen beantworten sollte:

1) **Ort:** Wo findet das Ereignis statt?
2) **Zeit:** An welchem Tag und um wie viel Uhr findet das Ereignis statt?
3) **Personen:** Wer ist involviert?
4) **Zusammenfassung:** Was denkst du über das Geschehene?

ACHTUNG

Erstelle einen Schreibplan, bevor du den Bericht schreibst, damit du nichts vergisst!

Beim Schreiben des Berichts ist Folgendes zu beachten:

➜ Die Ereignisse werden in der **richtigen Reihenfolge** aufgeführt.
➜ Man verwendet das ***simple past***, um über Ereignisse zu berichten, die in der **Vergangenheit** passierten.
➜ Jeder Bericht benötigt eine **Überschrift**.

Ein Bericht besteht aus **drei Teilen**:

1) **Einleitung** (***introduction***): Wann? Wer? Wo? Was?
2) **Hauptteil** (***main part***): nähere Beschreibung des Ereignisses
3) **Schluss** (***conclusion***): eigene Meinung zu dem Ereignis

WRITING A REPORT

1. a) Create one mind map for each topic below in your exercise book.

My last school trip

The greatest day of my life

My greatest holiday adventure

b) Create a writing plan for a report on one of the topics. Use your mind map and the tips from the explanation card.

c) Write a report based on the writing plan.

d) Read your report again and correct your mistakes.

EXPLANATION: WRITING A BLOG ENTRY

Mithilfe eines **Blogeintrags** erreichst du Leser auf der ganzen Welt. Deshalb bietet es sich an, den Eintrag auf **Englisch** zu verfassen.
Der komplette Blogeintrag ist **informell**, also umgangssprachlich, geschrieben. Auch Abkürzungen dürfen verwendet werden.

Der Blogeintrag besteht aus folgenden Teilen:

1) Über dem Blogeintrag steht immer der **Name** und das **Datum**.

2) Danach folgt eine **Überschrift** (***title***), die das Interesse der Leser weckt.

3) Mit der **Einleitung** (***introduction***) gibt man den Lesern einen ersten Einblick, worum es in dem Text geht. Die Einleitung kann mit einer **Frage**, einem **Erlebnis** oder einem **Zitat** beginnen.
   Have you ever been to a fantastic movie park? I have and it was great!

4) Im **Hauptteil** (***main part***) teilt man seine **Gedanken**, **Ideen** oder **Erlebnisse** mit den Lesern und gibt eventuell Tipps.

5) Am **Ende** (***end***) **bedankt** man sich für das Lesen des Blogeintrags und gibt einen **Ausblick**, worum es in dem nächsten Eintrag gehen wird.
   Thank you for reading my entry. I will tell you about my visit to the zoo the next time!

WRITING A BLOG ENTRY

1. a) Create one mind map for each topic below in your exercise book.

A trip to London

Computer games

My trip to the USA

b) Create a writing plan for a blog entry about one of the topics. Use your mind map and the tips from the explanation card.

c) Write a blog entry based on your writing plan.

d) Read your blog entry again and correct your mistakes.

EXPLANATION: GIVING ADVICE

Giving advice bedeutet übersetzt „einen **Ratschlag** geben“.

➜ Häufig gibt man Freunden Ratschläge, manchmal auch über eine **Mail**, einen kurzen **Brief** oder eine **Nachricht** auf dem Handy.

➜ Bei dem Verfassen eines schriftlichen Ratschlags ist es wichtig, dass man sich die Aufgabenstellung gut durchliest und den **Aufbau der jeweiligen Textsorte** berücksichtigt (*letter*, *email*, *blog entry* …).

Dennoch besteht ein Ratschlag aus **drei Teilen**:

1) **Einleitung** (***introduction***): Man benennt das **Problem** und zeigt **Verständnis** dafür.
I understand that you feel unhappy about moving. But we will find a way to stay in contact.

2) **Hauptteil** (***main part***): Man benennt zwei bis drei **Lösungsmöglichkeiten**.
I think we should …/If I were you I would …/It would be a good idea to …

3) **Zusammenfassung** (***conclusion***): Man erklärt, welchen **Lösungsvorschlag** man am besten findet, und **verabschiedet** sich.
I think it is best to …/I hope that I could help you!/Give me some feedback soon!/…

GIVING ADVICE

WRITING

1. a) What could your best friend do? Collect ideas for each problem in your exercise book.

1) Your best friend has to move in the summer holidays because his/her father is starting a new job in London. He/She is scared that you won't be able to stay in contact.

2) You and your best friend have planned to meet up with other friends next weekend. Your best friend got a bad mark on his/her last maths test, and now he/she is not allowed to come which makes him/her very sad.

3) Your best friend fell in love with a boy/girl from another class and is scared to tell him/her about it.

b) Create a writing plan for an advice on one of the problems. You have to write a letter to your friend! Use your ideas and the tips from the explanation card.

c) Write the advice letter.

d) Read the letter again and correct your mistakes.

EXPLANATION: STRUCTURING YOUR OPINION

Bevor man seine **Meinung** zu einem Thema in einem **Aufsatz** darstellt, sollte man gut überlegen, welche Meinung man in dem Aufsatz vertritt.

➜ Deshalb ist es sinnvoll, **Argumente für** (***pro***) und **Argumente gegen** (***contra***) das Thema in einer Tabelle festzuhalten.

Is homework helpful?	
pro (Argumente für Hausaufgaben)	***contra*** (Argumente gegen Hausaufgaben)
➜ *You get extra exercise every day.* ➜ *You don't forget everything so quickly.* ➜ *It shows you if you understand the topic well.*	➜ *If you don't understand the topic and can't do the homework, you will get a bad mark.* ➜ *Sometimes homework takes up too much time.*

Es ist sinnvoll, in einem Aufsatz die Meinung zu vertreten, für die man die **meisten** und **besten Argumente** findet.

STRUCTURING YOUR OPINION

1. a) Find pro and contra arguments for the topics and write them into your exercise book.

Gaming more than two hours a day has a negative influence on the school career of a student.	
pro	**contra**
➜ …	➜ …

The use of mobile phones in school should be allowed.	
pro	**contra**
➜ …	➜ …

b) Mark the best arguments and decide which opinion you want to represent.

EXPLANATION: SUPPORTING YOUR ARGUMENT

In einem Aufsatz, in dem man eine Meinung darstellt, sollte man jedes **Argument unterstützen** beziehungsweise **verstärken**. Um ein Argument zu verstärken, bieten sich folgende Möglichkeiten an:

Eigene Erfahrungen/Erfahrungsberichte
I think that doing your homework daily is the best preparation for a test. I experienced that with my last maths test. I did my homework every day and it helped me a lot because I didn't have to study so much for the test anymore.

Wissenschaftliche Studien
Studies have shown that doing homework regularly helps the students to understand the topics much better. Students who had to do homework got better marks in the tests than students who didn't have to do homework.

Berichte aus den Nachrichten
News all over the world can't stop reporting about the „HW-School". This school has an extraordinary concept. Every student who wants to attend the HW must sign a contract which says that he/she is willing to work on homework for at least 60 minutes a day. As the news report, the concept works very well, and all the students get better marks ever since they have attended the HW.

Beispiele (Diese können auch erfunden sein.)
If I do my homework, I can see if I understand the topic or not. This gives me the chance to ask the teacher for an explanation if I didn't understand something well.

SUPPORTING YOUR ARGUMENT

WRITING

1. Find a support for each argument and write it into your exercise book.

1) Playing computer games for more than two hours a day has a negative influence on my school career because there isn't a lot of time to study for tests then.

2) Mobile phones can help students learn better if the students are allowed to use them in the classroom.

3) Mobile phones in school should be allowed because most students communicate with their families and friends by using their mobile phones.

2. Look at the topic below. Find one pro and one contra argument for the topic. Then find a support for each of your arguments. Write your arguments and their support into your exercise book.

All students should wear a school uniform	
Pro:	Contra:
Support:	Support:

EXPLANATION: DISAGREEING WITH AN ARGUMENT

Gelegentlich muss man auch einer **Meinung widersprechen**. Das heißt übersetzt „***disagree with an argument***“.

Um einer Meinung zu widersprechen, sollte man zunächst **Argumente sammeln**.

A school year abroad is a waste of time.

No, because …

No, because …

➜ Jedes Argument sollte **unterstützt** beziehungsweise **verstärkt** werden.

Folgende **Satzanfänge** können dir dabei helfen, einem Argument zu widersprechen:

Englisch	Deutsch
I don't think so because …	Ich denke das nicht, weil …
I'm of the opinion that …	Ich bin der Meinung, dass …
A disadvantage is that …	Ein Nachteil ist, dass …
I disagree because …	Ich stimme nicht zu, weil …
I think differently because …	Ich denke anders darüber, weil …

DISAGREEING WITH AN ARGUMENT

WRITING

1. Disagree with the arguments. Try to use the useful phrases from the explanation. Write your arguments into your exercise book.

1) Smoking is good because you always find other smokers who you can talk to.
2) All computer games should be allowed for children who are 12 years old.
3) The school cafeteria should only sell fast food.
4) Every family should have a dog.
5) Students should have only four weeks of summer holidays.
6) Learning English in school is senseless.
7) Homework is not important for students.
8) Schools should start at seven o'clock every morning.
9) Fast food must be forbidden.
10) Children under the age of 12 years should not have their own mobile phone.

EXPLANATION: STUDY TIPS

VOCABULARY

Das **Lernen von Vokabeln** spielt eine wichtige Rolle, wenn man eine Fremdsprache lernt. Damit du erfolgreich lernen kannst, findest du hier einige nützliche **Tipps**.

1) Suche dir eine **ruhige** und **aufgeräumte Lernumgebung**.

2) Sorge für möglichst **wenig Ablenkung**, indem du dein Handy weit von dir weglegst und alle Elektrogeräte wie Fernseher und Computer ausschaltest.

3) Nutze deine **Lernpausen** sinnvoll. In deinen Lernpausen solltest du das Benutzen deines Smartphones, das Spielen von Videospielen und Fernsehschauen vermeiden. Versuche, an die **frische Luft** zu gehen, dich zu bewegen oder ein wenig auszuruhen, bevor du in die nächste Lernrunde startest.

4) **Wiederholung** ist das Wichtigste! Nur was wir wiederholen, speichert sich in unserem **Langzeitgedächtnis**. Versuche deshalb auch, alte Vokabeln regelmäßig zu wiederholen.

5) Probiere **verschiedene Lernmethoden** aus, bis du herausgefunden hast, mit welcher Methode du am besten lernen kannst.

STUDY TIPS

1. Answer the questions. Write the answers into your exercise book.

1) Where is the best place for you to study vocabulary?
2) Where should you put your mobile phone when you study?
3) What should you do during your break?
4) How many times do you repeat the words?
5) How can you remember the new words best? What's your method?

2. Study the new vocabulary by using the study tips.

castle	=	Schloss	outside	=	draußen
museum	=	Museum	camping	=	campen
city centre	=	Stadtzentrum	mountains	=	Berge
photos	=	Fotos	countryside	=	Landschaft
weather	=	Wetter	insects	=	Insekten

EXPLANATION: USEFUL PHRASES FOR THE CLASSROOM

Je mehr Englisch man im **täglichen Gebrauch** hört und spricht, desto schneller lernt man die Sprache. Deshalb ist es wichtig, dass man auch im Englischunterricht möglichst viel Englisch verwendet.

Hier sind **nützliche Sätze** für den **Englischunterricht**:

Englisch	Deutsch
What does the word … mean?	Was bedeutet das Wort …?
Could you repeat that, please?	Könnten Sie das bitte wiederholen?
I'm sorry. I don't understand.	Es tut mir leid. Ich verstehe es nicht.
Could you help me, please?	Könnten Sie mir bitte helfen?
Excuse me, is that correct?	Entschuldigung, ist das richtig?
Could you explain that again, please?	Könnten Sie das bitte noch mal erklären?
How do you spell that?	Wie buchstabiert/schreibt man das?
Where can I find more information about this?	Wo kann ich mehr Informationen darüber finden?

USEFUL PHRASES FOR THE CLASSROOM

1. Write the correct English sentence for each situation into your exercise book.

1) Du bittest die Lehrkraft darum, das Thema erneut zu erklären.
2) Du fragst einen Mitschüler oder eine Lehrkraft nach einer Übersetzung für ein Wort.
3) Du bittest die Lehrkraft oder einen Mitschüler um Hilfe.
4) Du möchtest wissen, wo du mehr Informationen zu einem Thema finden kannst.
5) Du verstehst eine Übung oder Erklärung nicht.
6) Du bittest höflich darum, dass etwas wiederholt wird. Hierbei kann es sich um eine Erklärung, eine Aufgabe oder ein Wort handeln.
7) Du möchtest wissen, ob du die Aufgabe richtig bearbeitet hast.
8) Du möchtest wissen, wie man etwas schreibt oder buchstabiert.

2. Study the useful phrases for the classroom.

EXPLANATION: DIFFERENCES BETWEEN BRITISH AND AMERICAN ENGLISH

In einigen Bereichen gibt es **Unterschiede** zwischen dem **britischen Englisch** (BE) und **amerikanischen Englisch** (AE):

1) In der **Aussprache** (*pronunciation*):
Beispiel: Während im britischen Raum das „r“ sanft betont wird, wird es im amerikanischen Raum gerollt und dadurch stärker betont.

2) In der **Rechtschreibung** (*spelling*): Einzelne englische Wörter werden im britischen Englisch anders geschrieben, als es im amerikanischen Englisch der Fall ist.

Beispiele:

BE	AE
colour	*color*
centre	*center*
organise	*organize*

Flagge Großbritannien

3) Einzelne **Vokabeln** (*vocabulary*): Bei einigen Vokabeln unterscheidet sich das ganze Wort.

Beispiele:

BE	AE
university	*college*
holiday	*vacation*
flat	*apartment*

Flagge USA

4) In der **Grammatik** (*grammar*) (jedoch nur minimal)

DIFFERENCES BETWEEN BRITISH AND AMERICAN ENGLISH

1. Answer the questions. Write the answers into your exercise book.

1) How do British English (BE) and American English (AE) differ from each other?
2) Find ten words which are completely different in British English (BE) and in American English (AE).
3) Find ten words which are spelled differently in British English (BE) and in American English (AE).

2. British or American English? What do you think? Copy the words below into your exercise book and write BE for British English or AE for American English next to them.

humour	______	humor	______	apologise	______	apologize	______
neighbor	______	neighbour	______	travelled	______	traveled	______
license	______	licence	______	dialogue	______	dialog	______

EXPLANATION: COMMON VOCABULARY IN BRITISH AND AMERICAN ENGLISH

Hier ist eine Auflistung einiger **Vokabeln**, die im britischen Englisch und amerikanischen Englisch die **gleiche Bedeutung** haben, jedoch unterschiedlich sind.

British English (BE)	***American English (AE)***	***German***
bin	*trash can*	Mülleimer
biscuit	*cookie*	Keks
car park	*parking lot*	Parkplatz
chips	*(French) fries*	Pommes Frites
wash up	*do the dishes*	Geschirr spülen
underground/tube	*subway*	U-Bahn
petrol	*gasoline*	Benzin
boot	*trunk*	Kofferraum
flat	*apartment*	Wohnung
toilet	*bathroom/restroom*	Badezimmer
garden	*yard*	Garten

COMMON VOCABULARY IN BRITISH AND AMERICAN ENGLISH

VOCABULARY

1. Copy the table into your exercise book and fill in the vocabulary. Write the German translation next to the British and American vocabulary.

yard	flat	do the dishes	trash can
underground/tube	car park	gasoline	wash up
toilet	trunk	(French) fries	chips
biscuit	petrol	cookie	bin
boot	parking lot	garden	apartment
bathroom/restroom	subway		

British English	American English	German

EXPLANATION: 25 / 5 METHOD

Die „***25/5 method***“ wird häufig angewendet, um effektiv lernen zu können.

So funktioniert die Methode:

1) **Arbeitsplatz** vorbereiten:
   - ➜ Suche die einen **ruhigen** und **aufgeräumten Ort** zum Arbeiten.
   - ➜ Lege alles bereit, was du zum Lernen benötigst (Vokabeln, Papier, Stifte …)
   - ➜ Zudem benötigst du einen **Timer** oder eine **Stoppuhr**, den/die du in die Nähe deines Lernortes legst.

2) **Lernphase** (25 Minuten):
   - ➜ Stelle deinen Timer auf 25 Minuten ein und starte ihn.
   - ➜ Nutze die 25 Minuten, um konzentriert **ohne Ablenkung** zu lernen.
   - ➜ In der Zeit kannst du die Vokabeln laut oder leise lesen, abschreiben usw.

3) **Pause** (5 Minuten):
   - ➜ Stelle deinen Timer auf 5 Minuten und mache eine Pause.
   - ➜ **Trinke** etwas, **bewege** dich ein wenig oder mache die **Augen zu**.

Wiederhole die *„25/5 method“* **zwei-** bis **dreimal**.

25/5 METHOD

VOCABULARY

1. Use the "25/5 method" to study the vocabulary below.

English	German
adventure	Abenteuer
rock climbing	klettern
sports	Sport
(to) go swimming	schwimmen gehen
(to) ride a bike	Fahrrad fahren
(to) go skiing	Ski fahren
dangerous	gefährlich
(to) do sports	Sport machen
(to) travel	reisen
guided city tour	Stadtführung

2. Repeat the method with the vocabulary from your English class.

EXPLANATION: WORD MAP

Unter einer „***word map***“ versteht man eine **Wort-Landkarte.**

➜ Hierbei beginnt man, alle **Begriffe** aufzuschreiben, die einem zu dem jeweiligen Thema einfallen, und erweitert diese **Wortsammlung** durch weitere Begriffe, die man mit **Unterthemen** des Hauptthemas verbindet.

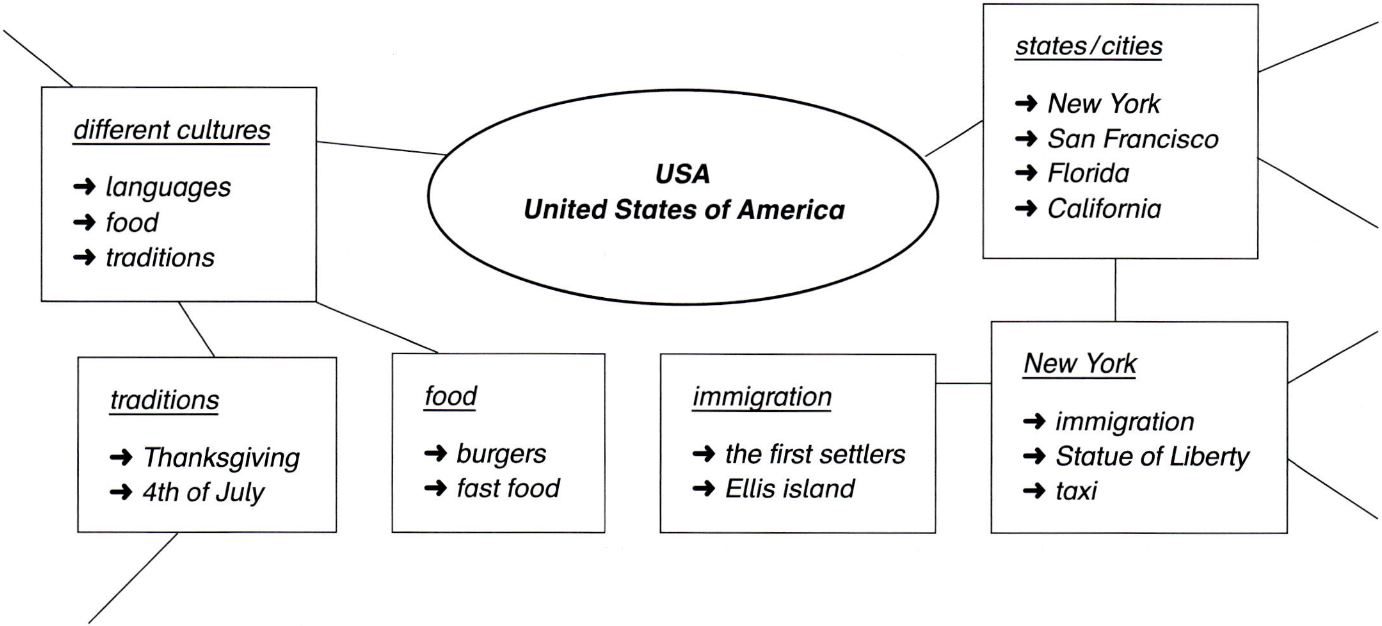

➜ Es ist sinnvoll, eine solche *word map* für **jedes Thema**, welches im Unterricht behandelt wird, zu **erstellen** und **abzuheften**.

WORD MAP

1. Create a “word map” for the topics below in your exercise book.

1)

The British Isles

2)

Living in the USA

EXPLANATION: RECORD – PLAY – REPEAT

VOCABULARY

Je häufiger man eine Vokabel hört, sieht oder schreibt, umso besser prägt man sie sich ein.
Deshalb ist die **Methode „*record – play – repeat*“** besonders gut geeignet, um Vokabeln zu lernen.

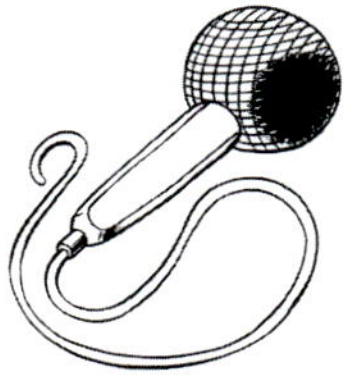

So funktioniert es:

1) Teile die Vokabeln in **Päckchen** von jeweils 10 bis 20 Wörtern ein.
2) **Spreche** dir das erste Päckchen **laut** vor und **wiederhole** diese Übung drei- bis fünfmal.
3) Öffne die **Audioaufnahmefunktion** auf deinem Handy oder Tablet oder nimm dir ein Diktiergerät zur Hand.
4) Lese die Vokabeln laut vor und **nimm dich dabei auf**.
5) Wiederhole dies mit allen Vokabelpäckchen, welche du lernen sollst.
6) Nun kannst du dir die **Aufnahmen** beliebig oft **anhören**, sodass sich die Vokabeln gut einprägen.

➜ **Tipp:** Führe die Methode zusammen mit Freunden durch.

RECORD – PLAY – REPEAT

1. Follow the instructions to use the "record – play – repeat" method.

1) Find a quiet spot where you can work.
2) Practice speaking the vocabulary out loud three to five times.
3) Open the recording app on your smartphone or tablet or take out the voice recorder.
4) Record yourself speaking.
5) Listen to your record until you know the vocabulary well.

vocabulary "food"	
English	**German**
food	Essen
yoghurt	Joghurt
health	Gesundheit
pasta	Nudeln
disgusting	eklig / widerlich
delicious	köstlich
cut off	abschneiden
cook	kochen
mix	vermischen / rühren
boiling	kochend
stir	rühren
add	hinzufügen

Digitales Zusatzmaterial inklusive!

So gelangen Sie ganz einfach an das Zusatzmaterial Ihres Produkts:

Wenn Sie das Produkt im AUER-Webshop oder in unserem Partner-Webshop Lehrerwelt gekauft haben, finden Sie das Zusatzmaterial in Ihrem jeweiligen Benutzerkonto unter der Rubrik „Meine Zusatzmaterialien".

Sollten Sie diese nicht finden, gehen Sie bitte wie folgt vor:

1. Rufen Sie die folgende Internetseite auf: www.auer-verlag.de/zusatzmaterial

2. Wenn Sie schon ein Benutzerkonto im AUER-Webshop haben, loggen Sie sich wie gewohnt ein.

3. Haben Sie noch kein Benutzerkonto? Registrieren Sie sich einfach und kostenlos.

4. Geben Sie Ihren persönlichen Downloadcode ein:

   U26187sEt

5. Laden Sie das Zusatzmaterial herunter.
   Klicken Sie dazu ganz einfach auf den Button „Download".

Möchten Sie Ihren Download zukünftig erneut herunterladen, so finden Sie alle bereits bestehenden digitalen Zusatzmaterialien in Ihrem Benutzerkonto unter der Rubrik „Meine Zusatzmaterialien".